THE RAVEN CHRONICLES

The Fight against the world crime league

by
Michael E. Morgan

The Raven Chronicles
The Fight Against The World Crime League

For information write to:
Dawntrader Books, LLC
PO Box D7-413
North Scottsdale Road
Scottsdale, Arizona 85266

If you are unable to order this book from your
local bookseller, or Amazon.com, you may order
directly from the publisher.
Quantity discounts for organizations are available.

Thanks to Zacarias Pereira Da Mata
for cover background

Cover and book design by
Michael E. Morgan

Publisher's Cataloging-in-Publication Data

ISBN 9-780990-3133-5-9
10 9 8 7 6 5 4 3 2 1

Table of Contents

The white culture has labeled the Native American Indian many things immigrating to the North American continent from Europe. Perhaps the descriptive language used might suggest more of an emotional reaction based on fear of survival as opposed to a practical observation of another culture. I warrant those negative feelings sometimes, as some tribes definitely exhibited savagery is certain. Thievery was also among their traits, but other tribes well knew those traits. Some tribes were fierce and savage-like in their fighting and lack of mercy of any kind. Other tribes recognized them.

There are many Native American tribes that have myths and legends that tell many things regarding the history and culture of the tribe. Sometimes, there are other aspects of the native culture that are kept secret, especially from outside cultures like the white man's culture. Travesties dealt to the many nations of Native Americans were tragic. The tribal elders are still bound to the old traditions and still fight against injustices, but in court these days. The secret heritage of these tribes speaks to the knowledge of the forbidden, the field of experience normally attributed to brujos or witches.

The culture of white people had religious beliefs and moral standards by which they wrote laws to govern their society. So, the Native peoples had their religious beliefs, though not directed at a specific God. These beliefs revolved around the energies of the world that surrounded them; the air, earth, fire, water, and Father sky. They overlook and watch out for the tribe. While Mother Earth supplies them with food, shelter and horses, that gives the tribe the ability to follow the migrations of the great buffalo herds.

Some outsiders have gained the trust and confidence of tribal members. As a result, they extracted a few details about the supernatural components of the Indian perspective, especially regarding the influence of spirits on daily life.

The supernatural world, also called the Shadow World, is full of many beings, both good and bad. The Indians live their lives embracing the Shadow World as an equal part of their life. They make all of their activities reflect on how the spirits favor their actions or not. The white man ignores the wisdom of his spirit sensibility, but only thinks about appeasing his god on Sunday mornings.

The 'Earth Mother' can be a savage and pagan idea. Without contemplating and embracing the Indian's view, they assumed to correct the 'savages' by supplanting their belief with a fierce devotion to a Christian ethic and dogma. The passion, devotion and honor of the white man are not so personal as it is with the Indian. White man's passion is validated by conquest and servitude. Instead of living life in harmony with the world and nature, the white man tries to manage, alter, or otherwise control nature to suit his own ends. The white man does not respect nature but believes he should try to master and subdue it. The Indian does not control nature but understands how to co-exist and live in harmony with it.

Why are these or any other indigenous peoples, that are not technically advanced, assigned this savage image overlay of their culture? This prejudice and violent rhetoric still obscures the true spiritual character of the Indian culture. The real rift between the white settlers and the Indians came mainly from their mistrust of the white man's 'truth' that became lies and the betrayals that created many broken treaties.

The modern conservative argument suggests Indians are takers, eternal welfare recipients that don't work or contribute to American society. This racial and separatist view is also inclusive of all races of color. The maledictions of Native Indian frustration are anger and sadness coupled with depression, anxiety and despair. There are a high number of homeless suffering with rampant alcoholism. So, the racially biased assumption prevails that a 'perceived' primitive culture would never develop a high degree of spiritual understanding.

The white man has no satisfaction. His attempts to dominate the world via aggression, genocide, bloodshed and destruction are all spawned by greed, fear and a lack of self-esteem. White man's world contains a seething hive of scum and villainy. The seizing of the native people's land by immigrating whites was political.

They systematically eliminated the threat of the Indian Nations rising against them through major military campaigns. They forced them into reservation camps that had little or no food, water, and even power for their homes. This is how they slowly exterminate the tribes by allowing them to wither and die off. Now, the rest of these people, burried in alcoholism and despair.

We almost lost the answers to deeper spiritual questions of Indian Culture through the rapid and systematic genocide of entire Indian Nations native to North America. Although the Native American population is dwindling throughout all tribes, there is still an effort to maintain the traditions and knowledge held sacred by the elders. They pass on this sacred knowledge to the younger generation with the hope for a better tribal life in the future.

One such tradition involves seeking guidance for a particular task or situation by using an underground covered pit called a kiva or sweat lodge, complete with hot rocks, steam and spirit-smoke, to encourage a vision from the spirit world. These ceremonies were sacred and usually held in secret, at special places often high in the mountains known to be frequented by spirits of the Shadow World. The participant seeking guidance, then ceremonially prepared to enter the kiva, led by a tribal shaman or medicine man. Even the medicine man himself can undergo this ceremony while he seeks spiritual advice to help guide his tribe.

Of all the Native American Indian tribes in North America, three particular tribes stand out as the fiercest among others in the southwest. The great Sioux Nation led by Sitting Bull, a great chief who fought many wars. Sitting Bull was most famous because of one great battle won at Little Bighorn, a strategic blunder by General Custer, resulting in the army's slaughter. Then there was the great Seminole Nation uprising, led by chief Osceola. Then finally, there is the Chiricahua Apache, who fought several wars against Mexico and the US Army. Among the Apache chiefs, two noble warriors arose, Geronimo and Cochise, who fought together. The San Marcos reservation was the habitat for most Apache Indians. The Seneca lake trading post was their principal source of sustenance.

An Apache tribe's medicine man at San Marcos, Jlin Litzoque (aka Yellow Horse) went to the trading post one day to exchange some of his tokens for food and supplies. The trading post manager harbored ill feelings about the Apache. The Apache were savages as far as he was concerned. He sought every opportunity to cheat the Indians in any way he could. He arbitrarily altered the exchange value of tokens and kept the difference to himself. Jlin challenged him about his behavior. Then the manager drew his gun, pointing directly at Jlin's chest. Jlin reached into his pouch and tried to bring forth an exchange rate notice to prove the manager wrong, but then the manager became angry and shot Jlin in the chest. Then, after, he planted a knife from the post showcase in Jlin's hand to offer proof of his thwarted attack.

The post manager ran to the front door for help to yell out to the braves nearby. The braves suspected foul play. When the gun went off, there were no witnesses. After checking his vital signs, they removed Jlin's unconscious bleeding body from the store without a word. They quietly placed

Jlin on the back of their supply wagon and headed for the occupation grounds of the reservation.

Their concern was to reach Nascha (aka Owl Woman), the only registered nurse that could handle Jlin's wounds. Later, the truth of Jlin's assault would be silenced forever when he died of internal complications. Owl Woman could not stop the internal bleeding.

News of Yellow Horse's demise spread quickly amongst the tribe. By tradition, one is chosen by the elders and a confirmation by Yellow Horse to assume his place in the event of his death.

Ka-e-Te-nay's son, Nantan Lupan, (aka Grey Wolf) was just 4 years old. After being observed by the elders, they found him worthy. Nantan Lupan was chosen. His future station in the tribe became fixed.

As a young boy, he dreamed of being a great warrior, not a medicine man. He wanted Yellow Horse to live forever, but that fateful childhood wish would not hold. Nantan's dream of leaving the reservation and San Carlos' corrupt ways seemed further away now. Gray Wolf was 23 years of age and passed the rightful age to enter the kiva trials.

One day, Gray wolf's father came to him while he was working on an old Chevy pickup that hadn't run for years. Gray Wolf could feel his father's intention long before he arrived. His father rounded the corner of the porch and stopped to sit on the battered, unpainted steps. He took a crumpled cigarette from his pocket and lit it up.

Gray Wolf interjected a criticism. "Those things will kill you one day, pop."

His father gazed upon another beautiful sunset debuting in the western sky. At that moment, he was unmoved by his son's critique. Then Ka-e-Te-nay mused.

"The light of a medicine man lights the way for the tribe, leaving hope in its wake. Think about the sunset, my son. Its decline shows a weakening of the light. Your denial of your responsibility is like the sun fading into the horizon. For our tribe, we need a strong spiritual leader who can assure the tribe the sun will rise again and shed its light upon the tribe and the elders for another day."

Gray Wolf's anxiety heightened as his father

continued.

"Our medicine man, Jlin, died at the brutal hands of a white trader many long years ago! The tribe cannot be without our spiritual guidance to help us through difficult times. Our tribe is blind now. We direly need a medicine man. It is time, my son! Yellow Horse and the Elders chose you, Nantan, as the successor, and perhaps even Jlin's avenger. Now you must prepare yourself for the ordeal of change. The kiva is being prepared as we speak. So, leave your duties behind and prepare yourself, my son.

Gray Wolf Looked into his father's steel-grey eyes and declared with a powerful voice.

"No father! I claim the right to challenge this ancient and useless tradition. To honor you and the wishes of Jlin, I will submit to the trial of change. In fact, I welcome it!"

His father bowed his head in disappointment. Despite Gray Wolf's statement, he felt his son to be weak-hearted. Nantan's father gave his last advice.

"Nantan, your grandfather fought along-side

Cochise at Apache Pass and again at Pikachu Pass. I am saddened that you reject your Elder's wishes while turning your back against your ancestors. I only hope that through your trials, you will learn to see the truth of this.

Meanwhile

In the world at large, evil continued to spread into other cultures and countries and developed into a giant malignant organism that ensnared the world with a vicious cycle of deceit and tyranny. I knew it as The World Crime League.

The agony of endless tyranny gripped the hearts and minds of millions of innocent, hard-working people who had relinquished their individual rights to choose in favor of safety and security. They allowed their fear of personal or financial harm to give way to extortion and protection racketeering. While they live subdued by these injustices, they cried out for justice.

The Shadow Kingdom heard the cries of the downtrodden. In the Shadow Kingdom, there are invisible beings that oversee the balance of forces on the Earth. The invisibles expressed concern at witnessing the extreme ravages occurring on the land. Nature was out of balance. They intervened and stop this tyranny and restore the balance of Nature in the world. This action required those that could move between the Shadow World and the physical world. They would be powerful, fearless warriors that could confront evil at its heart and render its collateral effects in the physical world harmless. Thus, justice and harmony get restored to the land and its people. Then the streets would become safe again for the children. The Shadow World would seek to recruit those worthy of this sacred but difficult task.

All the while, dark forces continued to gather. In 1992, a civil war began with the Triads participation against the revolutionary army of the Maoist Loyalist Cabal which attempted to overthrow the Chinese Communist Party and revert China to Maoism, and in the process became allies of the corporations based in Hong Kong and the Peoples Liberation Army in China.

During this period, their cooperation facilitated a new expansion overseas, allowing them to move their enforcers, mules and prostitutes into other nation-states as refugees. This expansion also caused conflicts to arise with other crime organizations over control of turf and encroachment of their own operations.

The Triads vary in their style of organization. Some are more loosely tied together, more like coalitions of gangs. They heavily structured the larger Triad groups with hierarchy with specific ranks with a council of board members.

They assigned numerical codes based on Chinese numerology to those members to define their rank. At the top of this Triad hierarchy was the Shan Chu, the lodge master or Dragonhead, who is numerically 489. He or she had brief contact with the rank-and-file members. Kwok Wong Sung was the ruthless leader holding the top rank of Shan Chu, but with his second in command, a woman held the top rank of Fu Shan Chu, or Deputy Lodge Master, noted by the numerical code of 483. She was Kwok's enforcer and known throughout Hong Kong as the Dragon Lady. She handled the day-to-day operations.

Below the Fu Shan Chu were two 483's of equal rank, The Heung Chu, or Incense Master, who was to enforce the traditions of the Triad and the Sin Fung, or guardian who was in charge of recruitment.

They taught members of the triad centuries-old hand signals and underwent initiation rituals based upon Taoist and Buddhist traditions and beliefs, usually ending in a loyalty oath to the Shan Chu. The last of the upper hierarchy was the Sheung Fa, or Double Flower, who established new branches of the Triad.

Certain 483s were the Triad's officers. The military commander in charge of gangs was the Hung Kwan, or Red Pole 426. Wo Kwan Wing was the Red pole who led the gangs against the revolutionary army. He was aggressive and ambitious. He was furious when the Shan Chu ordered a significant retreat at a critical time of the battle. His order caused several hundred Sze Kau gang members involved in the assault on the Wu Dang province to be slaughtered.

The Shan Chu foresaw the ultimate political

ramifications of the assault that would eventually favor their competition, the Tongs, for business in Macau. Kwan was a good military strategist, but short on political savvy. Kwan lost his opportunity to rise in the ranks from a brilliant military victory. He believed the Shan Chu deliberately ruined his aspirations out of fear of Kwan's ambition. Kwan strongly believed in the ancient Chinese principle of 'you get to keep what you kill.' Now, Kwan became a sworn enemy of the Shan Chu, and quietly plotted his assassination.

The night air became crisp higher in the Mescal mountains. Sage brush and other vegetation appeared to glow a pale blue phosphorescence in the full moon's radiance. The rubble landscape of the Mescal mountain foothills rose slowly from the dirt road. The cactus, cholla and staghorn thinned out while larger boulders appeared further up near the tree line. A dark green forest of pine filled the air with an intense aroma of resin.

Gray Wolf chuckled to himself as he made his way up the winding path to the sacred kiva that awaited his arrival. He thought to himself, "even a white boy could find his way home in this moonlight."

He borrowed his friend's pickup to get to the base of the mountain on time. Gray Wolf, determined to keep his promise to his father and the Elders and go through the trials, weighed heavily on his heart. He prepared himself to do that out of a greater sense of honor for his teacher, his family, and the honor of the tribal elders.

Gray Wolf's breathing became labored. The altitude forced him to stop from time to time to regain his strength. He realized the altitude was rising almost exponentially while his strength was declining in the same way. The path narrowed and grew difficult to climb without the aid of rocks and shrubbery providing the leverage needed to ascend.

He paused once more and inhaled deeply. His nostrils flared slightly to acknowledge a familiar scent, traces of burning mesquite wood in the air nearby. He was getting close to the ceremonial site, and the sweat lodge.

It is customary to use the sweat lodge to introduce young boys into the role of tribal responsibility and adulthood. In certain special circumstances like this, a special time, a special place high near the shadow kingdom, a boy can become a man and a man can awaken to himself and all of creation.

Gray Wolf reached the summit of a nearby cliff. Down below, buried deep inside, a dirt mound rested on the kiva. The only way in was from the top. The opening presented a narrow ladder descending to the inner chamber. Blue gray smoke rose from the opening, venting from the fire which heated the rocks in the pit. The pit lay in the center of the floor.

The moon shone directly overhead, shining its blue light back into the opening. The view reminded him of early images of the three wise men following the star of Bethlehem. All the stories told to him by the circuit preacher visiting the reservation he thoroughly enjoyed. His stories about the warrior Jesus disappointed him when he refused to fight his enemies. He believed it was because Jesus had no courage and no passion to fight and mostly because he was a white man! As Gray Wolf grew older, he abandoned the ideas of the white man's religion.

The moon continued to illuminate his descent, making his path to the kiva easy. Gray Wolf knew the Mescal mountains well. He hunted small animals while he freely roamed ever since he was a young brave.

The trials of the sweat lodge are severe. Many brave warriors have succumbed to the difficulty of many days and nights in the intense heat. It is a heat like no other. The breath escapes the lungs, replaced by steam and smoke. One's death looms near and the heat is so hot. If you did not bow your head regarding the fire elementals, your nostrils consumed with fire that reaches into the lungs.

Even though Gray Wolf was determined to exit tribal life, he applied his determination to the ceremony at hand, with the same enthusiasm. He believed he could call up the shadow world and enlist the shadow beings to help fortify his convictions. This arrogance to presume their acceptance of his wish-desire.

They lined the immediate path leading to the sweat lodge with fresh tobacco bound with ribbons of different colors representing various spiritual forces. These became offerings to the noble spirit while coaxing a favorable response.

As the ceremony began, three drummers beat the skins with special rhythms representing Mother earth and Father sky, as the spiritual surrogate called on their help in the transformation and metamorphosis of Gray Wolf.

Twelve hours passed, leaving Gray Wolf exhausted. He tried very hard to hold his focus and attention on his intention. Another brave played a sacred flute. The melody lulled him into a trance-like state. He became dizzy and lightheaded. Darkness closed in around him like a great iris, shutting out the light. Then he suddenly heard the screech of a raven so loud, he thought the bird entered the kiva with him.

With the rise of the third morning's sun, Gray Wolf opened his eyes. Thoughts remained jumbled, rolling around like loose marbles, while his head felt tender in spots like he suffered severe beatings with a club. He tried to get up, and the pain in his head amplified enormously.

As he lay on the floor, his earlier intention became a new conviction. He could not explain how, but the raven spirit communicated to him clearly that his trial was over. The raven told him he needed to leave the kiva and the tribe immediately that his destiny lies along a different path.

Gray Wolf got dressed and exited the kiva. His father waited to speak with him. Gray Wolf said solemnly, "Father, the spirits gave me guidance.

They told me I should follow my heart and my intentions. I'm sorry, father, but I must go my own way. Today, I will leave the tribe of my ancestors, my family and the reservation. Today, my new life begins with a vision. It's a mystery father, and I am compelled to seek it out."

The next evening, Gray Wolf visited the bar and say goodbye to his friends before he set out on his journey. He found all of his friends; Juh, Red Sleeve, Taza, Diablo, Dahkeya and Loco. They sat around their favorite table, already on their third round of beers. Taza called out to Gray Wolf. "Hey brother, come join us. We have something to celebrate."

Gray Wolf smiled as he approached and yielded to the individual hugs they demanded. Diablo handed him a can of Coors, the group's all-time favorite brew. Loco couldn't wait to be the first one to tell Gray Wolf of their plans.

Loco began quickly, but Loco spoke very slow. He was desperate to tell their story to Gray Wolf before he's interrupted.

"Gray Wolf we've enlisted in the marines

together. There is a special program that we plan to enter. The rewards are great. If we get into the program and pass it, our families and our lives will change. We'll be important! We'll get to see the world. Dude! I don't know about you, but we've had enough bullshit on the 'res' to choke a horse. We have always done things together, right? Like we're a separate family. So, you see the marines. They talked some shit to us. I got to tell you bro, it's sounds good to me!"

Gray Wolf frowned at them. "You guys are crazy! You really think the army is going to give you a square deal after all the shit and more than a hundred years of treachery, we got dealt from the man."

Diablo spoke next. "Listen, I don't know about these jokers, but I don't want to spend another day around this place. I'm up for something different. The pay will be good and there is travel. So, I'm in. If it doesn't work out, well, there is always Halley's bar to come back to!"

Then Diablo fired a critique at Red Sleeve, laughing out loud. "Yeah, Red sleeve is as slow as

Loco is with talking. He'll be the first to wash out."

Then Red Sleeve retorted in defense. "Dude, I could outrun you when we were both little, little brother! So, just don't get in my way!" Then everyone sounded off with an "ooh" along with their laughter.

Taza then suggested. "Hey man, why don't you join us? It'll be just like ole times together. What do you say, brother?"

Gray Wolf felt their peer pressure to join in their activities, as it always was growing up. He was just a follower, not a leader. He was confused and didn't know exactly where to turn. Then he stared at the floor pensively. "You know guys, I want to join you, but I have to listen to the spirit voice and my vision."

Dahkeya commented. "So, little brother, you've seen. Well, that's fine and I respect that but, what makes you so sure that we aren't part of your vision?"

Gray Wolf conceded that the spirit did not specify how it would go, just that he needed to leave the reservation, as well as his tribal responsibilities, behind. Then Dahkeya pressed him further. "Come on dude, don't be an asshole! It'll be fun and we'll show the white boys a thing or two about how the Indians do things. Come on, he repeated. You already said you'd like to join us. So, isn't that yielding to your heart's desire?"

Gray Wolf looked down at the floor for a moment. Then tipped his beer bottle toward Dahkeya and said. "Well, brother, where do I sign up? Then he turned to the others and added with a broad smile, let's get this party started!" After he said that, all stood and clanked their bottles together, followed by an Apache war cry.

After the Army swearing in ceremony, Graywolf joined his friends for a brief chest slap together and a hardy 'hoorah.' Their brief celebration quickly ended when the sergeant ordered everyone on deck for roll call and boarding the transport that will take them to Ft Benning for orientation and the beginning of phase one of their ranger training as well as, their evaluation for acceptance which, is called the 'Darby' Phase, named after Camp Darby.

Fifty men, believing they were man enough, tough enough and perhaps mean enough to kill on command, stood together as rank and file, at attention, in front of a small white podium. The sounds made from squads of soldiers marching along the streets in front of Quonset huts sang military chants of courage and fortitude in cadence with their marching, echoed high in the air.

Then Lieutenant Colonel Hafferty stepped up to the platform and adjusted the microphone. He tapped on it twice to make sure of its operation. Then he straightened the left lapel of his jacket, exposing the left side filled with many medals.

They represented many battle engagements all over the world in both the Asian and European theaters. He gently brushed over the medals as though they collected dust from his office to the podium. But everyone knew he did this to every recruit group coming in. It was the colonel's way of quietly establishing his supremacy amongst all that raging testosterone.

When he spoke, his voice seemed soft at first, almost reverent, as though he spoke from a pulpit. He reviewed some regiments and their histories, glorious battles won, and of course, the long-standing traditions of honor and devotion the Ranger Regiments have exhibited over the years, serving so many administrations, through so many entanglements and wars.

After the speech, the men in Graywolf's platoon marched with their duffle bags in tow to a temporary holding area. There, they would meet their DIs (drill instructors), Master Sergeant Sully Kincade and First Sergeant Tripp Mulvane. In military jargon, these two would become the 'good DI and bad DI' instructor pair that work closely together to mold these raging young bulls into a tightknit group, working as a well-organized team of fighting machines.

Master Sergeant Kincade explained the ground rules and what was to be expected of the men during their training. First Sergeant Mulvane explained the three phases of their training, beginning with the 'crawl'. These two experienced veterans of war will wield absolute control over the lives of the platoon for the next 9 agonizing weeks until they make the cut or not.

Graywolf stood beside his friends, all lined up along the left side of the second row in the platoon. Kincade slowly began his tour of each soldier, giving each of them an intimidating once-over. He purposefully left behind with each one, a deep sense of dissatisfaction with their appearances.

He would determine intuitively determine the strengths and weaknesses of each by caustic interrogation and humiliation, while demanding absolute obedience. To an onlooker, this would certainly qualify for inhumane treatment, but this existence was the only reality for these soldiers.

Their choices have dwindled to only one option: to get through the program. When Kincade approached Graywolf. It began with a stare down. He peered into Graywolf's almost black eyes with an intensity and fierceness only bested by his grandfather's stare when he did something wrong during his training on the Res.

Graywolf leaked a small smile. This was a cakewalk for him. He could do this even without blinking for minutes at a time. Whereas, Kincade had met his match and was about to discover his facing of the toughest customer in the platoon.

Kincade's eyes watered, but before he yielded to blinking, he ordered Graywolf to the ground and demanded 50. That meant 50 pushups, marine style, clapping the chest with both hands before returning to the ground. While Graywolf pumped through his punishment for his arrogance, Kincade began an assault on him and his friends with a need to prove their worthiness to the platoon because they were 'redskins', not good ole American white boys looking to serve their country. Kincade set out to make it harder for them than the others, to prove they were not Ranger material. Kincade did not hide his particular brand of racism.

Kincade's education was basically high school with a few college night courses thrown in, but as a warrior on the battlefield, he was clever, keenly observant, a will like iron and nerves of steel when surrounded and outgunned. It didn't take long for him to realize the humiliation and constant abuse had little effect on the stubborn, arrogant side of Graywolf.

After talking it over with Mulvane, Sergeant Mulvane suggested a reverse approach. "Whenever you don't like what the Indians are doing, make the rest of the platoon suffer for their antics and behavior. The platoon will pull together to bring them inline, and you won't have to do a thing except moderate."

So, when Graywolf, or his buddies, showed any sign of disobedience or disrespect, the entire platoon got punished.

One night, just after lights out, the Indian contingent stood near their bunks, talking quietly while the rest of the platoon hovered at the other end, deciding how to handle the problem. Finally, one chose. Private Beeman quickly agreed. He was a farm boy from Iowa. He was stocky and muscular and a state champion wrestler. As he approached them, he stood towering over them and wanted to appear threatening physically. He addressed them sternly about their concerns.

Graywolf wanted to be the first to face Beeman, but Dahkeya stepped in front of Graywolf saying, "let me handle this, little brother." The others granted Dahkeya a nod of approval. They felt he was their best choice as their champion in a fight. He stood taller than the rest of their little clan.

Beeman focused on Dahkeya's nose and said. "You think you have what it takes to take me down, little Indian boy!" Dahkeya retorted. "absolutely white boy!" Then another private interrupted. "Listen guys, remarked private Hoyle, we want what you want, but if this is going to be a pissing contest, then both sides should agree on some terms."

If Beeman here wins this fight, then you guys have to follow our lead, but in the unlikely event that… uh, what was your name again?

Dahkeya frowned and said "Dahkeya!"

"Oh right, sorry. If Dahkeya wins, then we follow your lead. Agreed? Everyone nodded in agreement, but then Dakkeya pushed his fist against Beeman's fist to seal the deal. Beeman took off his boots and shirt, while Dahkeya just removed his shirt. He was already barefoot. The rest of the men formed a circle in the aisle between the bunk beds and the latrine. Beeman threw the first punch and missed Dahkeya as he swayed back and ducked. Then Dahkeya spun around and jabbed sharply into Beeman's ribs, causing him to drop to one knee. Dahkeya waited for him to rise again. Then he spun around quickly with his left leg out stretched sweeping Private Beeman off his feet.

Beeman growled and jumped to his feet. He lunged toward Dahkeya like a freight train, out of control, plunging both against the circle of spectators. At first, it appeared Beeman had Dahkeya at a disadvantage. He locked his legs around Dahkeya's waist and, standing, partially threw repeated punches to Dahkeya's face, expecting he would pass out or give in. But then Dahkeya reached up and jabbed Beeman at his throat with two fingers. Beeman caught Dahkeya's punch directly to the larynx. He pulled away, coughing and choking. Dahkeya stood over Beeman, now hunched over, still trying to get his breath. Then Dahkeya spoke. "You had enough, Indian Fighter?" Beeman raised his hand to yield while still coughing. Dahkeya reached out to take Beeman's open hand and helped him to stand.

"I did not strike you hard enough to kill, but hard enough to persuade you to stop!" exclaimed Dahkeya. As you can see, we Indians do not go down so easily, contrary to the stories of your history books."
Dahkeya's fighting performance disappointed Graywolf. He wanted Beeman taught a lesson. Dahkeya chided him and said. "This is a better way, little brother, for all of us."

***

Basic training continued for Graywolf and his friends. Graywolf successfully completed the first phase called the Darby crawl. Then his shooting skills revealed where he made marksman status on the firing range. His friends were not far behind his performance. Graywolf, though the youngest of the Indian contingent, he soon made corporal and platoon leader. The natural abilities of the Indians in fighting, and obstacle courses, soon set them apart from the rest of the platoon.

Graywolf was eager to go to the 1st battalion 507th infantry airborne school, or as the troops termed it as 'jump school'. He knew that once he completed jump training, he would be eligible to enter ranger training.

Not all infantry troops enter ranger school, for anyone of several reasons, but usually the Darby phase is the training where many do not pass and take the alternate path of normal infantry. All five privately decided that was the direction they desired. 'The redskin five' also expressed that they wanted to remain together until they all finished. The 'DIs (drill instructors) at each phase of the basic Benning training gave the Indians high marks and saw that they already functioned as a tight nit group within the platoon. At first, the instructors were resistant to separate the five from the rest because of traditional total group orientation. But their skills were innate and obvious to the rest. Jealousy soon turned to admiration by the rest of the platoon. All were content to allow 'the redskins' to lead the way, inspiring their greater efforts to get through.

Of the original fifty recruits, only 32 made it through the Darby phase. The redskin five were at the top of their class. Now it was on to jump school and the second phase, Called the Mountain phase.

To become a ranger requires endurance, stamina, intelligence, and mental toughness. The Redskins five possessed these attributes and more. They were determined and dedicated to reach their goal. They could not wait to say, "we, the redskin five rangers lead the way".

Mountain training was based out of Camp Merrill in Dahlonega in northern Georgia, conducted by the 5th ranger battalion and builds on small-unit tactics involving knot tying, mountaineering and platoon-level tactics. We evaluate them for both technical and tactical expertise and their leadership. We test the students to know all four battle drills, including medical evacuation, call-for-fire-drills, troop leading procedures and how to write an operations order.

Many students could normally withstand these rigors, but the lack of food and sleep imposed during the training causes mishaps and injuries. One student buried food all over the mountain training area and then caught, then returned to Fort Benning to start all over again. Another took sugar packets for coffee, which also got returned.

Graywolf and his team were used to bad or no food on the res. Sleep deprivation had little or no effect on them. Graywolf would often go on all-night vigils hunting deer. The Redskin five also had another advantage. Their natural balance and sure-footedness provided for them easy traversing of the mountain slopes. Climbing steep inclines and descending those inclines at night with night vision equipment and a thirty-five-pound pack including rifle or machinegun plus ammunition was a recipe for disaster for most through the rough terrain, but no problem for the Indians.

The Redskins five very often helped their comrades in arms on Mount Yonah. Fear of heights emerged from time to time among some, but the Indian contingent also generously gave encouragement to those who needed it. Rewards for successfully completing the mountain phase were downtime, allowing food from loved ones' care packages and contact with parents. The Indian contingent did not have these amenities available and stayed close together for their own support on the base. The proper reward, as far as they were concerned, was the advancement to the Florida phase, with swamps, heat and the ocean assault on Santa Rosa Island.

At one point, one student did not make the correct knot when they were belaying and abseiling. His knot came unraveled, but Dahkeya caught him before he fell three hundred feet to the rocks below.

They carried combat missions out against

conventional threats during both day and night operations as part of a four or five-day FTX(field training exercise). There is usually an aim which they can reach; cross-country movement, parachuting into small drop zones, as air assaults into small mountain-side landing areas, or a ten-mile march across the Tennessee Valley Divide.

At the end of the mountain phase, the bus whisked those who passed to a nearby airfield to conduct an airborne operation involving parachuting into the Florida phase.

We conducted the third phase at Camp James E. Rudder on Auxiliary Field #6, at Eglin Air Force Base by the 6th ranger battalion. Here, the students receive instruction on waterborne operations, small boat activity with small stream crossings upon their arrival. They carried many of these tactical operations out in coastal swamp environments to test the students under extreme mental and physical stress. The ten-day FTX is an sped up pace of extremely stressful raids, ambushes and urban assaults to accomplish their missions. Then the peak of this experience culminates with the extensively planned raid of the ALF's(the cartel) island stronghold. When the students graduate after returning to Fort Benning, the black-and-gold Ranger Tab pinned on, and permanently worn, above the unit patch on their left shoulder.

The Redskins five were standing around sharing their excitement when a captain approached them, requesting that they come to the commander's office for a briefing.
They all looked puzzled and motioned if all were required to attend. The captain showed they were all summoned. So, they all piled into the base commander's SUV, wondering what is going on.

The Captain told the five to wait in the outer office while he introduced their entry. Dahkeya entered first with Graywolf and the rest in tow. They appeared in a semi-circle, standing at attention before the commander's desk.

The Base Commander, Lieutenant Colonel Hafferty stood up from behind his desk and said.

"At ease, gentlemen. Congratulations on your

completion of Ranger training. I have good reason to set you apart from the others. You have proven yourselves in the highest exemplary fashion under the traditions held highest in the Ranger unit.

"I have just received word from the pentagon. An operation conceived to be critical to the security of the Nation and its allies they placed into our hands. This mission is top secret and we will deploy your team on this mission tonight. Your orders are being cut as we speak. You will learn further details about your mission when you are on board and away."

The redskin contingent looked at each other and smiled. This was exactly what they were hoping for and why they joined the Army. They saluted the commander and left his office, practically jumping up and down with excitement. They couldn't wait to get back to the barracks and pack their gear. Their adventure was only hours away. And they put their worst fears about being separated to bed this day. They were delighted to be the team picked for this special mission.

Graywolf and the others now poised in the kneeling position on the tarmac with their gear ready to board a helicopter that would take them to a C-130 transport destined for Afghanistan and the airfield at Bagram, approximately 11 kilometers southeast of Charikar in the Parwan Province.

Once on board the transport, Graywolf opened the envelope marked 'classified top secret-eyes only' documents. Cargo nets that attached to the aircraft fuselage created the seating on the transport, forming small hammocks. His comrades shifted their seat locations near Graywolf in order to hear him over the engine roar. He stared at the opening orders with a look of surprise on his face. He looked at his comrades in arms and declared.

"Boys, we are to infiltrate the Muslim hide out and target Osama Bin laden for elimination. Intel gives us his location in the caves of Tora Bora, a complex in the Spin Ghar mountains in eastern Afghanistan. We will travel to Kabul by Humvee and coordinate with CIA operatives there. The CIA will be our lead in the assault. Everyone raised their fist in a united gesture, letting out an Apache war cry.

***

Later, after the transport landed, the Indian contingent removed their gear quickly and loaded the military ground assault vehicle standing by, which was really a Humvee fitted with a fifty-caliber machine gun turret mounted above and reinforced armor on the side panels. With everyone's gear stowed in the back, all climbed in with Graywolf, giving everyone a once-over of approval before he climbed aboard. Taza manned the gun turret mounted above the cab, which he found difficult to remain seated because of rough and unexpected terrain of the road. Graywolf called out to Taza while, struggled to study the plan of their assault on his personal map lying in his lap.

"How is it going up there, Taza?"

Taza responded by chuckling. "It's a wild ride up here. You should try it, little brother."

Graywolf responded sarcastically. "Bumpy roads upset my stomach!" Then everyone laughed.

Then, without warning, there was a sudden and deafening explosion from beneath their vehicle. It was a roadside bomb. The blast lifted the rear of the vehicle off the road, pitching it violently forward and tilting the vehicle over. Crushing and killing Taza instantly. The blast penetrated the center of the floorboard, ripping through and tearing apart the bodies of Dahkeya, Loco and Diabalo, spraying pieces of their bodies and blood over the backside of Graywolf's neck and head. Graywolf was thrown from the cab through the windshield during its first vault. Graywolf's body lay crumpled in a heap of partially exposed broken bones. He peered through his own blood at the burning spectacle before him. The harsh realization rolled over him like a stone. All of his friends were dead! Then a sharp pain pounded against the inside of his skull. He passed out, thinking he will join his fallen comrades.

***

Later, the only survivor of the bombing was Graywolf, but he was in a coma and lay quietly in a separate ward of the military triage set up at the Bagram Airbase. His prognosis was critical. They patched him up but his coma continued. The military authorities were desperate to debrief him as soon as he awakened , if ever. In the meantime, his mission was to remain top secret and his survival was now a security problem for the military. The plan to assassinate Osama Bin Laden was a clandestine operation designed and advocated by the CIA. The failure of the mission was not to become public. I felt that officially they would declare Graywolf as missing in action. His identity removed, and all information classified regarding his continued sequestering.

The Army held a funeral at Fort Benning with closed caskets for the families of the fallen soldiers. The caskets were actually empty, and the Rangers added a twenty-one-gun salute along with the traditional passing of the American flags. After they covered the empty caskets, they removed and properly folded and handed them to the relatives. All went home sad, but proud of their sons, depicted as heroes of the Afghan war. Meanwhile, Graywolf continued in a coma for many years and was eventually moved to the Guantanamo Naval

Base Detention center.

They centered a strategy meeting of the Shan Chu and his immediate officers on the need for stronger ties to Macau and other regions in and around the south China sea. They chose a secret meeting place in Wan Chai, a prefecture of Hong Kong Island. It was a factory leased by the Triad, conspicuously to make tailored suits of silk, but it was a major distribution point for the opium trade and export.

Two black SUVs pulled into the empty lot in front of the warehouse. The Triad leaders remained in their bulletproof vehicles while two other SUVs loaded with soldiers exited their vehicles first to perform the reconnaissance protocol of the area. After a brief surveillance of the surrounding area, they motioned the area was clear of danger. The Shan Chu were the last to exit, but all allowed him to lead the way into the factory.

The group moved through the maze of sowing machines and cutting areas of the main floor where hundreds of women would work during the day, while below the main floor, accessed by a secret elevator hidden by a false moving wall in the rear, took the group down to the opium preparation area, past the poppy cooking and processing. The heroin processed in this plant exceeded hundreds of pounds per week, representing one-tenth of their total output from other plants. Market value of this plant's output represented two-hundred-fifty million dollars in US currency. The production area, also manned by women, dressed only in underwear, bras and face masks working behind glass enclosed cubicles. Here the working hours were twenty-four-seven, with rotating shifts of women every day.

In the production's rear area was a glass enclosed office space, ventilated with filters to keep out the dust from the production area. An oblong and oval-shaped desk fitted with 9 chairs accommodated all the officers and the Shan Chu. Just before the meeting began, all the officers greeted Sung with an identifying handshake which confirmed their rank, loyalty and acknowledgement of the Shan Chu. Kwok sat down first with his second behind him, the Deputy Lodge Master, working to remove his overcoat and placed it around his seat. All the officers then sat down after and offered several issues to discuss.

Meanwhile, another clandestine meeting was taking place nearby. Kwan's plan to take revenge on the Shan Chu was about to unfold. Three unmarked vehicles closed in on the warehouse. Kwan and his loyalist soldiers piled out wielding automatic weapons and openly fired on the guards standing by. Return fire from the Shan Chu guards wounded two of Kwan's men and killed one other. Undaunted by the resistance, they hurried into the warehouse. There, they met with more of Shan Chu's men. Again, a hail of bullets streamed across the suit-making area, destroying several sowing desks and killing some of Shan Chu's men standing in the alcove walkway above. Their bodies fell into large laundry bins full of uncut material. Their blood sprayed out like a hose onto the floor.

Shan Chu and his second, the Dragon Lady, escaped down a rear stairwell leading to an alley. A black sedan was waiting. Shan Chu allowed Dragon lady to get in first, but before Shan Chu could get in they shot him in the back. He thrust his briefcase into the Dragon lady's hands and said.

"Here! Take my satchel."

As he handed his briefcase to her, his fingers released the handle slowly. His body slumped to the cobbled street while blood drooled out of his mouth, making a small red pool before her now seeped into her white silk dress. With his last whisper, he made one more attempt to reach out to her. Using what little strength left to him, he clenched his fist around her sleeve and begged.

"Avenge me, avenge me!" Shan Chu repeated desperately. The Dragon Lady said with tears rolling down her face,

"Wǒ fāshì yào bàofù, my master, she said in her native Vietnamese."

The Dragon lady looked behind her to view the unthinkable out of the rear window. Her last sight of Shan Chu's body lay face down in the street while the black sedan sped quickly away safely into the night.

The Dragon Lady's tears welled up in her eyes, but soon turned to fierce anger as she addressed the driver. She spoke calmly but sternly to him, clutching a small automatic pistol inside her handbag. Now she did not know who to trust, knowing the knowledge of the secret meeting leaked. But by whom, she wondered.

"Take me to the temple! She demanded. And make your movements evasive." The driver nodded without talking.

As the sedan swerved around traffic, continuing to take alternate routes and back streets, she contemplated who their enemies could be, clearly, well informed and well prepared. Considering the boldness of this outrageous attack, were fearless of any reprisals that would occur. She knew she would need to leave Hong Kong for a while. She gathered her most trusted members of the inner group to plan a new strategy.

Her plans would have a far-reaching impact on their entire operation in Hong Kong, as well as their operations in the South China corridor.

Fortunately for her, one enemy soldier was still alive!

After the Dragon Lady returned to the temple, her second suggested that she may still be in danger and recommended she go immediately to one of their safe houses. She considered this for a moment. Then she realized that they probably compromised all the safe houses. She decided additional bodyguards were necessary until she could get to the heart of this treachery. Under the temple was a secured area accessible by only one entrance and exit. This would be her refuge in the meantime. The Chan Shu would use this secured room when clan wars were happening in years past. She was confident that this temporary facility would suffice for now.

She ordered the prisoner brought to an interrogation cell, though wounded but not Fatally. Her soldiers brought him into the cell but not before making sure he had no way to commit suicide by cyanide, or some other method, thus to avoid this situation. They strapped him to a chair designed to tilt backward, offering his whole body ready for torture.

The soldiers began the process by keeping him from resting and randomly turning the lights on and off. After 48 hours of no sleep and frequent water torture, he revealed his allegiance to Kwan, the leader of the attack. Then they slit his throat. It did not surprise the Dragon Lady to hear the results of the interrogation. Her intuition suggested long before, a sense of ambition and disloyalty within Kwan to the Shan Chu. She needed to understand why he would choose boldly attacking before she ordered a response to his treason.

She stared at the door of the secured room, reflecting the countless number of times she had entered this room to help the Shan Chu develop a strategy during the clan wars. She entered the pass code and the door unlocked and slid back into the wall. It felt strange to sit down at the Shan Chu's desk. She plopped the briefcase in front of her. Opening the briefcase reminded her of a childhood experience she had secretly gone into her father's personal things.

She smiled with a brief grin as she pulled all the confidential folders, contracts and other documents regarding other clans, and of course the code book, revealing the account numbers and banks that related to the entire operation. For her, it meant she was now Shan Chu.

Three days after they brought Graywolf's body back to the Bagram Airbase, the darkness seemed endless and swallowed him. It was pure blackness with no detail. Then, from time to time, he would experience a waft of cold air breeze past him. He chalked it up to his imagination or, worse, his death trauma.

He couldn't be sure that he wasn't dreaming what he saw and felt. At one time, he thought he could hear voices. The voices were faint and far away. He could not make out the words, just jumbled sounds and intonations. He ignored them, hoping for something more.

Mentally keeping busy, he tried to embrace this vast blackness while reconciling the fact it may be the only view of eternity. Actually, while many negative thoughts crossed his mind relating directly or indirectly to his present circumstances, there was one exceptionally great thing he realized. He still had a mind he could think of!

He couldn't feel his body, despite many attempts to do so. But he considered, perhaps, having nobody in this 'afterlife' was payback for his insolence and rebellion to his father and to his tribe. Even these feelings and thoughts were fleeting and eventually ceased to have any significance.

Graywolf kept experimenting with what he was and where he was, looking for some kind of answer. It always came to nothing. He didn't quite give up but consoled himself by thinking, if there was a time where he was, he had occupied himself for the time being in this eternal blackness.

Then he wondered if he was tired. Could he sleep? Or could it be that he remains in this quasi-awake state tortured with questions that had no answers? He thought if he died, then where were his ancestors to greet him on this other side of existence?

Graywolf's consciousness had drifted out of his body without realizing it. Now suspended in the void's blackness, somewhere beyond his body.

Brief but violent images would crash through his mind like a runaway train. Images of his friends dying on the road to Kandahar. Severe pain rushed through his consciousness, weighing on him like hot lead pouring through his veins. His brain seemed to swell beyond the walls of his cranium, on the verge of exploding with tremendous pressure. Then the pain suddenly stopped. Graywolf remained suspended in the darkness, hanging now, dazed and confused.

Far ahead into the darkness, a dim light emerged. He squinted to see what seemed to be something growing larger. He realized he could not avoid whatever was approaching, and he seemed to be the object of interest. The shape now taking form in front of him, not yet defined. It moved nearer to him, appearing sometimes like a man. Graywolf tried to identify him at least by his clothing, possibly as an Indian. Exactly what tribe the stranger belonged to, he could not discern. This stranger showed an unusual tribal dress, unrecognizable to him. The stranger's stance was clearly noble, such as a chief of a great tribe might stand. Then he reached out to make contact without success.

There was no answer as the face faded back into the blackness. Then Graywolf tried to cry out in his mind. Just as that desperate thought passed away from, again there was someone moving toward him. It was an indiscernible shape but yet seemed to stand out as a slight difference in the shade of black against an even darker background. The shape kept changing as if it were developing into something bigger, taller. The shape would approach, then recede. With each movement, it developed into something more. The object loomed closer and suddenly a man appeared again and stood before him, smiling. Graywolf was happy to see something, someone, anything besides the eternal darkness. He called out in his mind.

"Grandfather". Is that you? Please don't go!"

Graywolf felt relieved that he might have someone to talk to and spoke from his mind again.

"Who are you? Can you tell me where I am, and am I dead now?"

The entity stood before him, not speaking, but keenly observing him. Now Graywolf studied the entity more carefully. He was tall. There was a feathered ploom jutting off to one side of his headband. His shirt-tunic was a deep red with small flowers imprinted all over and adorned with three quarter-moon-shaped gold plates dangling from his neck. He seemed to hold a staff with many eagle feathers draped loosely from the top. As Graywolf stared, he wondered if he was dreaming. He reached for his eyes to rub them, but the movement was not immediate, making Graywolf doubt whether he had a body. He felt himself sort of groping to find his face. Just when he was about to give up, suddenly his hands covered his face. He rubbed vigorously as one might if washing the face in ice-cold water. He blinked twice, catching several flashes of dim light.

There was a ringing in his ears. He tried to stop it by sticking a finger inside his inner ear. The ringing continued, but the annoyance ceased to be an issue. The returning vision of the Indian in front of him distracted him. He stared into his black eyes and heard a low voice speaking. Graywolf sighed in relief that he spoke English.

"Graywolf, be still and listen. Your ancestors

have requested my help to help you complete your Nagual training. I am Osceola, Master Nagual and Spirit Chief to the Seminole people. I am to be your teacher and guide in the shadow world."

Graywolf tried to speak. He wanted to, but no sound came from his lips. Trying with all his might, he again and again could not make a single sound. Frustrated, he retreated from the struggle. Then he thought.

"Have I died and returned to the land of my grandfathers?"

Osceola responded with a slight smile. He lifted his hand in a gesture to halt Graywolf's pathetic efforts to struggle with his vocal predicament.

"No little brother, you are not dead but you are apart and deep asleep. While your body slumbers and continues to heal your wounds, we will begin your training in the shadow kingdom.

"You will learn to navigate this place in time and you will find your voice, eventually. The laws of reality here do not function in the same way as they have accustomed you to the earth."

Graywolf struggled to hold back hundreds of

questions burning like searing embers and trying to break from his prison of silence like a herd of wild horses. He soon realized that Osciola peered into his mind and spoke to him directly.

"Rest your mind for now. Know, my brother, that your destiny is about to unfold. For now, allow yourself the opportunity to listen and broaden your understanding."

Graywolf turned and bumped into something. He reached out with his hands to touch the obstacle. It seemed vague at first, round like a barrel but perhaps conical, rising near where he was. He turned in another direction and he bumped into another object, this time with his head. It hurt for a moment with a dull ache. He felt the shape of the new obstruction. It also seemed round and conical, but in the reverse, hanging down above him.

He blinked twice and caught more flashes of dim light. He became still for a moment. The darkness faded into a pale-yellow band of light that spread before him. Details of objects turned from gray shadows to solid objects. His view continued to widen to a large cavernous space with some stalagmites and stalactites nearby. Now he was more bewildered.

Osceola said.

"Right now, we have brought you to a lower astral chamber of the earth. This place will harbor and facilitate everything you will need for your training. This place will always be where you will come when called to perfect your skills. It will be to you as Ah-Tah-Thi-Ki, a place for you to learn. When you need to come here, just utter those sounds and you will arrive.

Osciola brought before Graywolf the first of five challenges that he must endure before he can begin his training. Then everything around Graywolf became still.

Osciola spoke again.

"There are five areas of difficulty you will face: jealousy, anger, arrogance, pride, and Fear. In each case, I will soon introduce you to circumstances where you will have to face each one of these elements and find a resolution to each dilemma within yourself. You must discover if the strength of your character suffices to overcome these pitfalls, thus proving your worthiness of the wisdom you are about to receive should you succeed.

Each period proceeded regularly, one after the other, as a normal night and day would pass, yet it all proceeded as a continuation of the darkness in the shadow kingdom. To Graywolf, it felt as if he were awake and living in this strange place. He felt incredibly vulnerable in this new world, bringing back memories of his training as a young boy on the res. Now left to this stranger for his comfort and solace, as his father provided in the past.

The lessons learned in these five experiences are that Graywolf discovers that each experience is unimportant but his reactions are more important and that he needs to see and accept his reactions while letting go of the incidents that created those reactions and understand how each reaction when resolved becomes the element of change in his character for him to proceed.

The Dragon Lady now functions as the ipso facto leader of the Hong Kong Triad. She sits at the desk of the late Shan Chu, pondering her dilemma; quietly assume command or show a sign of power and merciless force to instigate fear in those who would challenge her right to rule.

She felt uneasy about considering the passive approach, considering the amount of treachery she witnessed at Shan Chu's second. They must do publicly the upsurge of need for gratification from the elimination of those who conspired to assassinate the Shan Chu, most brutally. Then suddenly she felt an inner resolve, a new sensation of inner strength to become her destiny, the supreme clan ruler of the south China seas.

She invited all the clan leaders to a summit meeting. As a gesture of confidence to move forward and create new alliances of all the clans, to develop new strategies for mutual benefit for all, but her actual intent was to determine who could or would be involved in the Shan Chu's treachery.

Not all attended her invitation. At the moment, this was of no concern for her. She could still reveal the truth from those who attend. Dragon Lady knew that her invitation would be unacknowledged if it did not also embrace the traditional way. An important gathering would require that the Shan Chu would assign a date that corresponds to an important festival. Her choice was to meet during the month of April, coinciding with the Ching Ming festival.

That festival begins in fifteen days, which gives her plenty of time to prepare her plans for a 'Saturday night massacre' for her honored guests. It will also give her time to prepare her speech and proposal to the member clan leaders that survive.

She prepared a banquet table that was long to accommodate everyone's seating Arrangements. Meanwhile, she had constructed a false center in the middle of the table to place her assassins waiting at her beck and call while hiding quietly inside.

The time was near six o'clock when everyone would arrive. She took the normal precautions with armed soldiers placed strategically for her protection. All attending members disarmed at the door as a matter of mutual respect. Dragon Lady missed little in any situation, which is why the Shan Chu chose her as his second. She considered the off chance someone would want to take advantage of her 'apparent weaknesses' with the Shan Chu gone.

The location was semi private. She secured one of her restaurants, the Chang Li Palace, with only the chef and crew present. They were under guard and kept away in the kitchen.

The Dragon lady retreated to the upper management office and opened a secret panel behind the bar. There she kept a potion concocted by her daemon consort to give her clairvoyance and the ability for a short time to see the truth of another by just gazing upon them. Drinking some of the potion quickly, she restored the bottle back into its hiding place. She descended the stairs and suddenly felt dizzy. She remembered some of the side effects of the potion and waited for the initial reaction to stop.

After everyone got seated, she raised her glass to offer a toast to the unification of all clans working in harmony together for their mutual concern and benefit. She stressed the importance of loyalty, and that loyalty is now rewarded with the shared profits and their shared protection. Everyone seemed to nod in agreement and some murmured concern how she would accomplish such lofty goals.

Dragon Lady lowered her glass while she slowly scanned the room, looking for telltale signs of betrayal beyond the normal jealousy for her position. She looked for Kwan but he did not attend. Kwan sent his second, Cho Niang, with apologies. As she stared at him, he squirmed a little in his seat and offered a sheepish smile. Making no attempt to reveal her preemptive knowledge. No one else gave rise to suspicion. Then she gave the order to eliminate seat number 7, where Cho sat.

Suddenly, the center of the table burst open and her assassin emerged with a blast of automatic rounds into Cho's chest, his body slumped to the table lifeless with a thud. Cho's blood spilled onto the white linen tablecloth in a slow spreading pool.

The room still ringing from gun fire while everyone ducked to protect themselves. The Dragon Lady held up her hand to stop, and then the banquet room became silent.

She spoke solemnly but firmly for everyone left to sit down. They all complied willingly, while some continued to stare at Cho's body. All eyes turned to the Dragon Lady, standing quietly with her pistol in hand. She lowered the pistol and placed it strategically on the table in front of her. She leaned slightly forward, placing her hands on the table, and peered into everyone's eyes one by one.

She offered a slight wry smile at the corner of her mouth, quite pleased with the fear she created. Then she began.

"Okay. Now that we have eliminated the distraction, may I still have your undivided attention? Let us discuss the plan for reunification of all the clans in the corridor."

As she detailed the prescribed duties and responsibilities of each clan, she was confident about having already ordered another hit. Three of her best assassins arrived at Kwan's brother's nightclub. Two entered through the back entrance and the third entered the front of the building. It was still early, and the club had not yet opened for the evening's festivities. Kwan sat in the back of the main dance floor in a semi-circular lounge chair alongside his brother and two bodyguards. Kwan's sister was standing nearby laughing along with the others when the assassins appeared like ninjas. They executed everyone in a hail of crossfire into the group. Though the bodyguards had drawn their guns in response, all went down quickly without a fight. After, the hail of bullets stopped. One assassin walked over to Kwan.

His bleeding body draped half-conscious across the lounge on his back. He bled from his right side, left shoulder, and a grazed wound on his neck. His eyes were closed and his breathing labored. He reached to stop the bleeding from his neck. When Kwan opened his eyes and looked up, he saw the masked assassin pointing his Glock 17 nine-millimeter pistol at Kwan's head. His red laser targeting the sweet spot between Kwan's eyes.

Then Kwan's expression of desperation appeared briefly on his face as the assassin fired twice at point blank range. Two small holes appeared, surrounded by powder burns above his eyes. The exit points were not so neat. Those rounds abruptly tore out the back of his head, splattering blood mixed with pieces of his brain all over the booth table.

Confirming all were dead, their task was done. Then the three went out the rear entrance as quickly as they came. Once outside, one of them pulled a small cell phone from inside his bright red Michael Jackson jacket. He clicked the autodial feature and waited. A female voice answered softly. "Yes?"

"It is done, Shan Chu!" the assassin said in a low, affirmative tone.

"Excellent, she praised and went on. Go! She commanded. Leave the city at once. Make your way to our facility in Macau for now. Then you can return when I call you. Your compensation will wait for you there."

The soldier assassin responded.

"By your wish, it is our command, Madam Chu."

Meanwhile, she concluded her speech with everyone nodding in approval. All felt confident that business would continue to flourish as usual. The changes she intended to make did not strike anyone present as particularly unusual for a change in leadership. She showed to all that she could quite settle the score with her rivals with swift and deliberate action. Proving the Dragon Lady had a firm grip on the helm. With one swift blow, she secured her leadership of the Triad. Thus, began her reign as Supreme Chancellor, the grand Shan Chu of the South China Sea Corridor.

She would continue with her supernatural cohort, the silver fox daemon, to root out and destroy any remaining vestiges of resistance to her absolute rule over the organization. Her name would become infamous throughout all of Asia. Within a year, she had muscled in on the markets beyond Macau and successfully interfered with opium product routes leading into the United States. She secured footholds on the docks of both eastern and western shores by seizing control of their labor unions. As she promised, proceeds from the reorganization and the newly secured opium routes made profits soar.

She decided Macau would be the new hub of her operations. She moved the headquarters to an island province just sixty kilometers from mainland China. The last emperor of China, the PU-Yi and twelfth ruler the of the Qing Dynasty, established a palace fortress there as a retreat and defense against marauding pirates. With its ports affording her easy access to the west and the few renovations required, establishing greater security was relatively easy. Now she felt confident to sit beyond the easy reach of Hong Kong treachery.

After the release of the Portuguese jurisdiction in 1999, Mao's Revolutionary Government repossessed the territory of Macau, but left a small contingent of Portuguese to administrate. The fortress, originally called the Fortaleza De Monte in Santo Antonio, became a registered historical site. Before she came, it was a tourist attraction for the Chinese government. This minor nuisance was tolerable. Outwardly, the fortress functioned as a tourist attraction, giving her perfect cover for her operations. The mainland was kind enough to offer a regiment of soldiers to guard the perimeter of the palace-fortress, which kept her expenses down. The Portuguese administrators were keen to keep their positions and more than happy to assist in the extensive dock and port operations with no complications. It thrilled them to be on the Triad payroll, which bolstered their meager salary which, rarely arrived in a timely manner. Meanwhile, the Dragon Lady continued to consort with her evil companion, the Daemon Fox Baruto, whom she had made a blood pact with. She promised to eliminate Naruto, Baruto's nemesis.

Baruto, the fox, sought the coveted 9 tails chakra, an ancient supernatural artifact offering the possessor with enormous magical power. Up to now, Baruto could not defeat Naruto. Hirata, who received the nine tails chakra from the ancient sage of the six paths, Hamura. They killed him during a sorcerer's battle and passed the nine tails chakra to Naruto just before he died, making him a formidable opponent. The Dragon Lady's close alliance with Baruto fueled her boldness for expansion, both in the shadow kingdom and in the outer world.

Graywolf labored over his confusion about this strange world. Initially, he found it difficult to trust this being posing to be his teacher and guide. Despite Osceola's apparent familial knowledge of Graywolf's ancestors, he continued to keep his suspicions about whether Osceola was a friend or foe. His doubts regarding his new reality also could be a fantastic dream, or he was dead and suffering from afterlife hallucinations.

Then the sudden appearance of Osceola interrupted Graywolf's thoughts. Osceola looked pensive and appeared as though he were going to speak. He just stood in front of Graywolf silently for what seemed to be an eternity.

Just as Graywolf's curiosity had urged him to ask Osceola what he wanted, Osceola raised his arm and their surroundings completely dissolved into a dramatically different scene. Now they were both standing at the outcropping of some rocks overlooking a huge waterfall that seemed to fall into the oblivion of mist below, not allowing Graywolf to determine their altitude.

Osceola pointed to an aged foot bridge. Ropes

looked worn and even frayed in many places. The boards forming the path of the bridge were only forty percent present and most rotted. The problem was also to reach the footbridge. He had to climb down from the outcropping to even reach it.

Osceola seemed to be undisturbed by the obvious unsafe conditions and unsympathetic that he was asking Graywolf to cross the bridge, knowing full well he would never get across and that the attempt would be certain suicide!

Graywolf tried to evoke a sense of reason from Osceola, but to no avail.
He knew he didn't have a choice. The peak they were standing on was cracking and beginning to crumble away, leaving him on the shaky bridge as his only escape. He also had no time to think about options.

Just as Graywolf stepped onto the swaying bridge, the wind increased in velocity, causing the bridge to swing more violently. Then, as he took his next step, the board already appeared rotten and gave way under his weight, allowing his foot to crash through, leaving him dangling between the hand ropes.

Then he realized that for him to make it across, he would have to synchronize his movements with the timing of the swings.

His next step strategically placed on the side rope forming the walkway.
As much as this would have comforted him, in that same moment, he could see that the footbridge, not used or maintained for hundreds, if not thousands, of years. The foot rope showed that by the fraying and rotten threads exposed.

The sound of Oseola's words of encouragement grew fainter as he approached halfway. The ropes were all creaking under the stress of his weight and the extreme movement which now alarmed him. He would look down into the mist of the abyss below, alluring to his demise, if he should make one dangerous move.

He glared at the formidable remaining footbridge ahead, appearing more like a nightmarish taunt to die a horrible crushing death below. Graywolf knew if he let his mind get out of control and panic, doom lay ahead. With each step forward, he whispered to himself. The wind howled like a banshee with furious taunts of fear begging to turn around. He reasoned with himself that his odds of survival were better ahead. Though he knew it to be just as risky as turning around.

He was at the mercy of the integrity of the ropes, and they now seemed to give way to collapse. With that thought, there was a sudden snap followed by a hard jolt on the left, causing the footbridge to lose its form and twisted up with him caught inside. He looked for ways to climb out of this tangled net of ropes. It seemed hopeless at first. He tendered considerations of just letting go to the inevitable conclusion. His death was now staring him in the face.

Graywolf did not whimper or cry. Instead, he let out a warrior's yelp and, in that same moment of acquiescence, the other right foot rope snapped with another jolt.

The ropes binding him in the twisted net unfolded, leaving him dangling from the boards just above him. He wrapped one foot around the foot rope while the rope separated and Graywolf began a sudden swing downward toward the wall of the cliff on the other side. He tried to embrace and absorb the impact. But some of the cliff was an outcropping of rock and the impact, though mostly against his left shoulder, knocked him unconscious.

In his unconsciousness, he let go and minutes later awoke hanging upside down with only his foot, still intertwined in the ropes. He needed to regain his upright position before he could continue climbing. He was dizzy and disoriented from the blood rushing to his head. His vision was distorted and blurry. He kept grabbing for ropes that were not where they seemed to be. After many minutes of struggle, he righted himself, but was exhausted. Despite urges to keep moving, he stopped to rest. While he still dangled precariously from the ropes, he sat for a moment, taking some tension away from holding on for dear life. He was going to need all of his strength in his arms and legs if he was going to survive this disaster.

He closed his eyes to focus his inner will and empower his perseverance. There was one rope still crossed above him, offering the opportunity to get his hands on the other planks above. The rope he was aiming for was out of reach. To get hold of that rope, he would have to sacrifice his momentary position of relative safety and lunge for it. He felt his fear rising as he looked down into the mist far below.

He knew he could not stay where he was and eyed that rope with hope and aspiration that he would succeed.

He maneuvered his feet to free himself for his one and only chance to get out of this situation. Bracing against the rope he was standing on, he crouched as low as he could and leaped with all of his might. It shortened his upward momentum as his leap loosened the rope which anchored him. He slipped downward but got his right hand around his prize.

His right arm already fatigued and begged to be released. He knew his is life hung in the balance and it would be his right arm that could save him from the rocks below. At that moment, an ancient memory came to him. He was a boy and his father had turned him over to his uncle for training. His uncle was keen on making Graywolf strong and flexible and focused on pull-ups, especially one arm pull-ups. Then he smiled at the memory and gave thanks to the memory of his uncle, then he wondered if he would ever see his family again. Realizing that thought was debilitating, he cast it out of his mind with the affirmation he was going to reach the top of that cliff.

Now he focused all of his energy on his right arm and, though his biceps were straining, he pulled with all his might to bring his left hand in range to grab that rope. Then the first board above him was within reach. It was half broken already and looking very weathered, not worthy of his trust. Then he could almost hear his uncle's words; 'boy you don't want to consider the negative odds, spirit is your power, let go of it and let it carry you to your goal.'

Again, he smiled slightly, silently giving thanks for his uncle's advice. With a firm grip on that weakened board, he reached with only the tips of his fingers; he got hold of the next board. As he scanned the boards further above him, he could see that there was a definite quality improvement as they became more substantial further along.

His confidence grew with the mounting of his weight onto the next board until he realized he was closer to the ridge of the opposite cliff. There were two more boards to climb over before he could claim his precious goal and save his life. As he grabbed the second to the last board, it snapped in half, causing him to drop, but he grabbed the rope adjacent and save himself from a death provoking fall.

He warned himself not to get too cocky and reassured himself that his climb would end soon when he could reach solid ground. The last board proved capable of supporting his last thrust to the ground above. Throwing his left leg onto the edge of the cliff, he pulled the rest of his exhausted body to the safety of the ground. He laid quietly on his back and breathed easier. He felt thankful to his ancestors and his family for his current abilities and courage.

Oseola appeared before him, looking down at him with a warm smile.

"Congratulations! You have passed your first trial, young warrior. But you still have more challenges ahead of you. Now you must rest and prepare for the next trial. Then he disappeared. Graywolf felt mixed feelings, glad he could get past this trial but worried also about the other trials. Would they be harder for him? He wondered? Then he passed out.

Graywolf awoke to find himself again in the great cavernous space. He expected to see Osceola appear, but his expected arrival did not come. Loneliness settled deep into his heart. He wondered about his father and his tribe, while still not sure that he died and all of this was just an after-death fantasy.

Moments later, his father appeared before him. Graywolf could see that old look on his face. The look of disdain and disapproval. Then he spoke to Graywolf with great judgement and condemnation.

His father paced back and forth in front of him and exclaimed. "Now, do you see the outcome of your arrogance and self-willed attitude? Serving and thinking only of yourself." He punctuated with an exclamatory humph. And before Graywolf could answer, his father continued.

"Your refusal to serve your tribe in how they needed you caused this unfortunate calamity. You willingly led your tribal brothers into the jaws of death, for which there is no return! Unforgivable!"

Graywolf was speechless at first. His anger rose inside of him with every word his father intoned.

Like a great dragon, his heated breath burning through his nostrils while engulfing his heart with the pain and anger for their loss. He waited impatiently to explode in his defense.

Graywolf never felt his father's love, only his dissatisfaction with him. He felt he could never live up to his father's expectations for him. Even as a small boy, he pushed Graywolf harder, with no kindness or mercy. He struggled in defiance to play with the other boys of his age. His father demanded of him better performance with all of his activities while heaping more chores upon him. There was little time to enjoy his childhood games while the responsibilities of becoming a medicine man weighed heavily on his heart. He believed it was too much for him. The cruelty formed within him a cold and calculating spirit well beyond his tender age while on the Res.

Then, that memory reinforced his rejection of his father and his tribal commitment, forging with a strong feeling of resentment and spite. If he was dead to the world, he was happy not ever seeing his father's grimacing face again.

Now, convinced that seeing his father after his apparent demise revealed a just punishment for his past deeds and attitudes. Realizing then, he would spend all of eternity alone with his suffering. Lamenting with sadness, he would never join his ancestors in the 'happy hunting grounds' promised to all noble warriors.

But soon his anger returned with the full force of a phantom iron horse puffing and snorting its black smoke as it charged boldly across the prairie desert with a certain determination and disturbing violence to even the score.

Graywolf shouted at his father. "I Joined my friends in the war because they were already determined to join the army. In fact, they wanted me with them. So, he paused with a certain self-righteous indignation, you are wrong about me once again. As a warrior, I may choose how and when I will die. What I am doing with my life is my choice, not yours, or the wishes of a dead medicine man. I do not owe the tribe my life. That got decided without ever consulting me, or how I felt. I believe if he were here right now, the medicine man would agree!"

His father continued to chide him. "You were always a willful child! You were never willing to take on your duties and chores with a positive attitude. I had to make you do them at every step. Pushing yes, I wanted you to be the best above all others."

Graywolf broke into tears, exclaiming. "You just don't get it, do you? Can you not see? You are blind with your own ambition, vicariously living through me. When it is actually you who sought the perfection for yourself. You were trying to make up for your own shortcomings through me, your son!"

"Well, Graywolf said with finality, I am probably dead now and no chance for me to go to the promised land of noble warriors. I have led my friends into harm's way and they are all dead and as far as I know, I don't see them because they have died an honorable death while here I sit, tormented and cursed for my deeds. I hope you are happy now because I'm no longer available to kick around to suit your personal needs!"

Graywolf bowed his head, drowning in more tears. The sound of his father's voice faded. Osceola's voiced returned instead.

"Graywolf, you have carried this heartbreak for most of your life. You wanted very much to please your father, while resenting that he would hold out giving his love to you in return only when you deserved it from your best efforts. You quickly learned that his love would never come, only his scorn. He held your wish for his love and comfort over your head to manipulate your actions. This is how he controlled you to do exactly what he wanted. He was blind to his ambitions, as you were also blind to his maneuvering and intentions."

Osceola continued. "You must come to understand this recognition of his nature and realize he brought you his pain and suffering on his behalf. Your father was a weak man who dumped his weakness and guilt upon your heart to ease his own."

"Anger and resentment are attributes that can cause you to be off center and off balance in your actions. Your further development on this path must include coming to grips about this and letting go of it."

"You no longer need to depend on a love that will never come to fruition. Actually, quite the opposite! Now you must take in what you have said and what you have heard today to realize that you can move beyond this behavior. It no longer serves you. You have the strength of the wolf in your heart."

"You have the determination and willpower to function on your own with love and gratitude for yourself and your precious gifts. You must meditate on this! Your training will come to nothing so long as your heart is not clear and burdened with such negative energy. It will interfere with everything and contaminate your progress. It will eat away at your mind, giving way to sap you of your vitality and will certainly obstruct the right decisions at the most critical moments."

"There are greater enemies that still lie in wait ahead of you. Your training requires you to find out with certainty their skills and abilities. You must realize all their ways to deceive and beguile you to lower your guard. You need to cleanse these feelings from your being and replace them with your courage and forthrightness."

"We must guide your actions with a faith in yourself and what you are doing at all times. To accomplish this, we must make your heart pure. This will allow you the control your movements with precise accuracy and keen insight for the eventual unfolding of unknown forces. This path is a path of spirit and spiritual integrity. You not only must advance your martial skill beyond the physical realm, but you will need to control your feelings as well within the supernatural realm."

"Master Osceola, how am I able to do what you speak of? You speak as though I am still alive!" Graywolf declared.

Osceola smiled slightly at his remark and continued. "You are apart from your body. Your body lays sleeping while we take the advantage of a 'captured audience', meaning your mind and heart. The physical reality is not as secure as you might think. It is an obstruction to the right thinking about you and your true essence. You have absorbed wrong concepts about your so-called reality. What you think are your limitations and liabilities is simply an illusion. We are here to assist you in changing your perceptions and introduce you to the true reality of this world and many others' worlds beyond your imagination could ever conceive."

Graywolf sighed with some relief. "I was thinking I was dead to the world."

Osceola smiled again at Graywolf. Then he began again. "You are dead to the world you once knew. Now we will bring your consciousness into the light of true reality and introduce you to the forces of darkness that are harbingers of evil and seek to dominate the world you knew with their manipulation and control. The level of darkness is on the rise and seeks to control human actions in the world you knew before. You have a very important part to play in all of this."

"I will leave you now to meditate and process what you have learned today. You are tired and need rest for the other trials you will face."

Graywolf unknowingly fell asleep. When he awoke, he was sitting on a rock near where the boys of the tribe would hang out. He noticed several of the boys huddled around another boy. It was Dahkeya his rival. He left the rock and parted the group to get a better view of the group's interest.

Dahkeya brandished a new knife his father gave to him. He wore it proudly in a new tooled leather sheath bound to his waist. Dahkeya was the tallest. He used his size to help embellish his leadership. Graywolf was a little shorter than the rest and suffered for it. Dahkeya would often challenge Graywolf by threateningly showing his dominance. Graywolf was not afraid of him, despite the enormous differences in their stature.

He had tangled with Dahkeya on two previous occasions and he quickly found he was no match for Dahkeya's strength, speed and agility. The first time it was over a cute girl named Dyani. She spoke little, but like a tomboy, preferred to hang with the boys whenever they allowed it. Her coal black hair, loosely braided, would hang well below her waist. Graywolf often liked to watch Dyani and admired her anonymously. As she ran to keep up with the others, he enjoyed seeing her locks of hair sway gracefully from side to side.

She liked Graywolf, but was too shy to reveal her true feelings. She seemed impressed by the bombastic and energetic Dahkeya, the designated leader. He approached Dyani aggressively and made romantic gestures while taunting Graywolf with inflammatory remarks. Unlike Graywolf, Dahkeya always showed a certain confidence. Everyone wanted to be his friend and followed him.

Dyani's apparent interest in Dahkeya confused him. He exploded with rage and jealousy. Graywolf, without warning, suddenly lunged at Dahkeya in a full-frontal attack. His humiliation in front of Dyani became a struggle for his honor and dignity. He ended up on the ground under Dahkeya, now saddled squarely on his chest. Dahkeya administered several punches to his head and chest. Graywolf lay bleeding from his left eye and nose. His blood dripped down the front of his shirt.

Afterward, satisfied he sufficiently crushed his

opponent, Dahkeya got off triumphantly. He walked away laughing along with the others. Meanwhile, Dyani rushed to Graywolf's side, offering her scarf to wipe away the blood, but he was too embarrassed to accept her offer.

Hurt, he believed himself to be the better man. He could not understand her poor judgment in choosing Dahkeya. It made him feel inadequate. His failed attempt to win her feelings with his daring, but the fumbled assault continued to fuel his anger. He pushed her hand away, exclaiming, "leave me alone!" He could not see beyond his blind jealousy that she catered to Dahkeya only to win his approval to hang with the boys and to be nearer to Graywolf.

Graywolf's father would often admonish Dahkeya as a shining example of strength and courage. While shoving Dahkeya's prowess in Graywolf's face, declaring his disappointment in falling short of his expectations.

The second time he tangled with Dahkeya, he pushed Graywolf to the ground, declaring he was too puny to be a great warrior like himself.

Graywolf became so angry and frustrated that he picked up a rock and threw it as hard as he could, taking aim at Dahkeya's overgrown ego. He struck his mark as David might have struck Goliath, right across the temple. It dazed Dahkeya at first. Stunned, that Graywolf's accuracy surprised him.

He stomped toward Graywolf with a grim determination to even the score. Just as he grabbed his collar to exact revenge, Graywolf turned and pulled away, sweeping his foot just behind Dahkeya's left leg. They both went down. Before Dahkeya could beat him senseless, Graywolf's father interceded in the rising conflict. Sending Dahkeya back to his home while he took Graywolf inside for further punishment.

Graywolf took his punishment without shedding a single tear. He was so jealous of Dahkeya. Sitting in silence after his punishment, he refused to reveal his true feelings. He felt lonely and abandoned by his father's misunderstanding. As he sulked, he longed for the day he would seek to leave the Res for good.

Suddenly, the scene faded from view, leaving

only Osceola Standing before him. Osceola commented.

"Your feelings of jealousy and envy weaken your spirit. They make you awkward and clumsy. Dahkeya served a greater purpose here; to reveal your underlying condition. You blindly sought revenge and ignored your true inner need for love and acknowledgement."

"This happens because you allowed your Tonal side (the physical unconscious brute) to outwit your Nagual side (the wisdom of your spiritual nature). In order to prevent this from happening, you must learn to search your first true feelings."

Graywolf looked at Osceola with a blank stare.

"I don't understand what you mean?"

Osceola continued.

"The brute can only react! Reactions are secondary feelings relating to the first true feeling, which you do not want to feel because that leaves you vulnerable. Your vulnerability does not make you weak. It strengthens you and is more alert. Your vulnerability is an asset and gives rise to your unified being."

Only the first true feelings can bring greater consciousness to yourself, which can nourish your spirit and keep you from losing your balance. The loyal warrior remains perfectly balanced, quiet, with the inner feeling of honesty, integrity and awareness in your relationship to yourself and your surroundings at all times.

"It allows for right action with precision and accuracy well beyond the limitations of unbridled reactionary feelings brought on by a false sense of yourself. You can only know your true strength from that place of solitude."

Osceola continued on.

"You cannot hope to master the skills afforded you with your Nagual training without first mastering your tendency to yield to your uncontrolled and unbalanced feelings. Your superior skills can only manifest when you flow from the silence within your being."

"The master of the Nagual calls forth the energy of clear insight, looking to future events that will assist in your effort to bring about a balance in the physical world. The darkness that lives within men to accomplish evil in the world, made by the infinite darkness of fear and the insistence on the use of violence and chaos to attain power. Not unlike nature that uses great power to bring a return to balance and harmony. Darkness is chaotic. It is truly weaker than the light. Confusion through misinformation and disorientation are just some of its tools to uncenter you. The darkness needs to create the fear in order for it to wield power to exist."

"A great storm rises to tear down and destroy what has become unbalanced. Though it momentarily disturbs the apparent peacefulness and tranquility of the established imbalance, it purifies and weakens the power invested in the chaos through the energetic equalizing effect of Nature's lightning, the power of the spirit, the Nagual, burns away the negative vibrations that corrupt goodness and sweeps away the contamination that breeds more evil."

"You will learn in time to master your feelings, to redirect that precious energy to focus more positively on the creation of greater light and love that encourages growth and understanding among men of the world.

"In the meantime, meditate on the truth of your true value, not coming from an outside verification source, but from the source of the noble spirit that supports life and the eternal evolution of greater consciousness that lies within you. But it sleeps for now. Soon the sleeper will awaken. Then you will come to realize, you are not of this crude matter you call your body. It is merely a shell by which the true being lives. Then you will move beyond the limits of the physical reality and flow with the Nagual into the true reality."

Graywolf then closed his eyes and re-entered a deep sleep.

Osceola looked upon Graywolf with fondness as he whispered quietly.

"Sleep well, my friend. You have further important inner work ahead of you. You will have need of your gathered strength."

Graywolf awakened to find Osceola standing nearby. He motioned for Graywolf to follow him into another passageway. It opened into a wide space, appearing as an arena for combat. Many members of his tribe surrounded the arena space as spectators to the ensuing battle about to begin. Graywolf hesitated. Before him was Dahkeya standing tall grinning from ear to ear with confidence about the outcome.

Osceola motioned to encourage Graywolf to engage. Graywolf looked at Osceola with less enthusiasm and greater doubt about his success. Then Graywolf questioned the meaning and necessity of this battle.

Osceola looked down for a moment with a certain impatience. He motioned again for Graywolf to engage. Then he spoke.

"We hoped you would learn from your experience with fear and apply it to this experience with the caveat that your perception of failure is to be altered here in this entanglement."

"Graywolf insisted. Where is there meaning in this? I see no point with this obvious display of unequalled strength between me and Daykeya. He has defeated me many times on the Res. Why now, and why here?"

Osceola smiled with a slight grimace.

"You have many misconceptions which need to be revealed through these trials. We hope you will learn about your patterns, which undermine your abilities to call forth and make use of the Nagual powers of spirit. These powers lay dormant deep within you, awaiting the call to action by the part of you who is now sleeping. You need to awaken that part of you. Fear rises within you, blinding you to your inner being. You don't like the feeling because it allows you to feel your inadequacy and then, to avoid that first true feeling, creates the very action in you that defeats you."

"It is your pride that replaces and defends your inadequate feelings from yourself. Battle is a perfect way to bring forth these imbalances within you. So, proceed."

As Graywolf approached Dahkcya, he circled him, hoping to increase Graywolf's insecurities. Fearing the rebuke of tribal members after the humiliation of his defeat clouded his mind with other considerations. He looked around for a weapon that could even see the obvious lack of his strength. Sweat trickled down his temples. Dahkeya then taunted him with some cruelty.

"What's the matter, little brother? You sweat and stink of fear from the apparent oncoming of your defeat and demise?"

Then, Graywolf replaced his fear of inadequacy with anger and embarrassment. Osceola commented.

"Now, can you see? Your reactions to his taunt cloud your inner strength and clarity of mind. Your reactionary feeling already weakens your position. Stop and consider your thoughts and feelings. Is it true what he is saying, or is there another truth that eludes you in this moment? Dahkeya is calling out your apparent weaknesses. It belittles you in your eyes and increases your distorted view of his apparent strength compared to you. Consider your strengths over and above your sense of inadequacy. Make that action your first challenge to him."

Graywolf bowed his head to consider Ocseola's advice. Graywolf tries to reach deep inside past his fear of the humiliation of defeat amongst his peers, while Dahkeya continued with his taunting.

"Look brothers! He said while he raised his arms to gesture support from the spectator crowd. Then he continued. See how he closes his eyes and bows his head in shame!"

Graywolf deflected that statement from inside and tried to move beyond it. Despite the taunting, he continued seeking for that substance of inner will and strength of being that Osceola spoke of.

As Dahkeya made aggressive moves toward his opponent, Graywolf be smaller and quicker, artfully dodged or slipped away from his attacks. As Graywolf plotted his best advantage, he moved in quickly to sweep Dahkeya off his feet. Dahkeya went down, but only partially. Before Graywolf could move in to tackle him, Dahkeya quickly regained his defensive stance. Meanwhile, Osceola commented on Graywolf's approach. Though Graywolf's tactics were initially impressive, Osceola criticized more about his inner feelings and how they affected his assaults.

Graywolf's anger continued to interfere with his

movements. Osceola revealed his weakest points while he defined his awareness at certain critical moments in his critique.

"You telegraph assaults and easily discovered well before you complete your approach. You must clear your mind and heart of these vengeful feelings and, above all, forget about your past performances." Osceola chided.

Graywolf turned briefly to acknowledge Osceola's advice, only to catch Dahkeya's quick punch to his left side and a swift blow from his elbow to the side of his head. Graywolf went down to his knees, trying to regain the breath just taken from him in the previous attack. His head buzzed with dizziness and his vision blurred slightly.
Meanwhile, Dahkeya continued to taunt him.

"Stay down, little brother, and conceded your defeat once again!"

Graywolf turned his vengeful feeling into laughter. Then he retorted.

"You won't take me so easily, brother, not this time! If you defeat me, it will change nothing. I will rise regardless of the outcome. I will learn from you the nature of your fighting skills and reveal to me some of your weaknesses. I can see now that you depend on your size and weight as your primary advantage."

Dahkeya smiled.

"Ah little brother, you act with forethought. That is good! It makes you a better opponent, but it won't matter. It gives me an opportunity to show my superior fighting abilities and squash your meager attempt at a fruitless effort to defeat the best warrior in the tribe."

Osceola commented again.

"Yes. He has greater strength and greater stature, but where are your talents best served in this case? Your size makes you faster and more agile. Consider how you might use his energy and strength to support yourself while applying them against his efforts to subdue you."

Just then, Dahkeya grabbed Graywolf's shoulders. Graywolf quickly dropped to a stooping position and reached for Dahkeya's ankles and gave a quick jerk. Daykeya toppled forward, leaving Graywolf standing over him. To this, he said with a smile while getting up.

"Oh! So, you have a little quickness in you little brother."

Dahkeya shifted his tactics and became loose in his movements, as though he were dancing around Graywolf. Graywolf braced for the unexpected as Dahkeya spun around now, attempting to sweep Graywolf off his feet. Graywolf sprung into the air and narrowly missing the oncoming leg. Then he swung around in time to catch Dahkeya's foot and flipped Dahkeya back onto the ground again.

Dahkeya grew tiresome of the taunt and became angry. He leaped back onto his feet and lunged toward Graywolf like a buffalo in a stampede. With almost psychic intuition, Graywolf moved aside just in time with the precision of a fine matador without a cape to cloak his movement. Dahkeya once again stumbled and landed face down.

Just as Dahkeya arose to yet another assault, he dissolved before Graywolf's eyes. Before Graywolf could speak, Osceola intervened in his mental confusion.

Graywolf, you have overcome your pride, learning to flow with your essence instead of defending yourself by hiding behind your pride. Your pride blinds you to yourself and to the reality of the outside world. So, as you can see, this shift has resulted in some of your gifts emerging within you. This can now make your skills as a warrior formidable.

In Brussels, Belgium, it is now 5 p.m. The sun rested for a moment at the western horizon, beaming its last golden rays into the Ministry of Foreign Affairs building. Hotel staff drew the shades of the conference room while the last of the members find their seat at the conference table. Then all leave who are not members. The double doors to the room are closed. The conference room remains quiet. A special meeting of the CGA (Committee for Global Alliance) began.

The CGA group, for all intended optical purposes, served as a global humanitarian relief organization. Various foreign dignitaries, key financial institutions from wall street, and parts of the US military Industrial complex sat at the table. Top scientists at Lockheed, Boeing, and NASA came forward from related research facilities funded by black budgets under DARPA (Defense Advanced Research Projects Agency). Los Alamos Labs, Cal-Tech, Monsanto Chemicals and other representatives from EST (European Science and Technology Center) at CERN, Switzerland, were also present.

The first subject high on the agenda, the emergence of the so-called World Crime League. The impact of their nefarious activities strongly suggested unexpected expansion and the serious erosion and destabilization of the world's economies.

The chairperson defined with great detail the vast destruction and mayhem brought on by these organized terrorists and their allies. When he finished, a clamor of discussion and debate began around the oval table. Each member possessed a secret identity known only to the organization as a delegate of a certain number.

Delegate number 11 from the United Arab Alliance called for a swift and wide-sweeping elimination of known League leaders masked as a Jihad clandestine war. Many agreed unanimously against his idea. The direct approach made up a major assault on many of the league's groups, perhaps costing CGA billions with no guarantee of success and the risk of exposure. The systematic and surgical elimination of crime league leaders, though desired, is theoretical for the moment. All basically agreed that such action would bring certain and unwanted attention to their own operations and, worse, the exposure of their clients.

Delegate number 7, from British Intelligence MI-6, offered another idea. Some backdoor contacts at the NSA (National Security Agency) informed him of an experimental program to develop special forces as an anti-terrorist task force. The program explored creating super soldiers that could be more effective than the notable seal teams now in use. Delegate number 7 was quick to add that as far as he knew, the program was only a feasibility study and no real developments came from the project.

Delegate number 9 from Lockheed then corroborated delegate number 7's story. He exclaimed it was a top-secret project, codenamed 'Nightshade'. He knew little about the details other than the program was active as far as he knew. Then delegate number 5 asked what was so different about this task force and the purported successes of seal team units used before.

Essentially, the idea of using a team of trained assassins became a plausible and favored endeavor. Everyone agreed the need was great and also urgent. The model suggested for this team of super soldiers would be the shadow warriors of feudal Japan. They would be a new adaptation of the legendary ninja, a long since abandoned and forgotten cultural oddity from Japan's history. Everyone agreed to move forward with the development and adoption of this new task force quietly dealing with the League's terrorist activity.

The energy and momentum became contagious even among the more conservative members of the council. Some members, eager to get started, suggested increasing black budget funding to ensure the success of their plans. Others suggested the need for a special facility or compound where such secret training can carry on.

A concern arose from delegate number 5 that there would be danger in centralizing the operation, as attractive and as simple as that might suggest. A well-funded clan of trained assassins could feasibly and discretely carryout seek and destroy missions to confront and defeat the plague of the World Crime League, but certain critical factors needed to be considered.

First, the idea of a clan of assassins knowing each other would defeat the purpose of complete anonymity, an essential part of the success of the operation. No agent should know the identity of any other. In this way, no one could betray, either consciously or unconsciously, the identity of any other members. Also developed is a discrete process to recruit additional members for the clan. Ideally, it would be those who have some fight training, such as members of the military. Preferably, those would be candidates already serving as, or had served in, the special forces.

The council decided all recruits must have their history and credentials cleaned from all data servers. Like some other agents in the field, they would wipe connections to family and friends and country of origin from their memory. Some felt this action too extreme, but eventually retired to the obvious conclusion about the necessity of anonymity. This worked best through a variety of military actions. New recruits, listed as MIAs, if captured and or killed by the enemy. Then replacement bodies, sent home in closed caskets for immediate burial.

Usually, new recruits are then rendered unconscious for days until they reroute their bodies through several organizations and their associations at continuously changing locations. They sent even those who come from the battle torn areas and return wounded to secret undisclosed hospital triages where their wounds cared for with no trace of medical drug use and or rehabilitation equipment needed for recovery.

There were tiers of combatants all having different specialties and skill sets, but they gave certain special psychic tests early to reveal innate talents for additional training and exposure to supernatural beings who could provide the knowledge and special methods that would apply to unusual circumstances. This involved the use of the occult to battle opponents who are also skilled in the paranormal.

With all the precautions taken for extreme secrecy, we give each recruit an invisible tattoo at the base of the neck just beyond the hairline. It appeared as a small flower defining their membership to the clan. It was only visible under the exposure of an ultraviolet light of specific frequency.

Each assassin carried a small pouch that contained many helpful items for their field work. One of those items was a small pen that would produce that special light once one slammed one end of the pen against a hard surface. This would start a chemical reaction needed to provide the power for the UV light for a period of only one minute before it self-destructed.

That concept kept the possibility open to confirm someone suspicious as a friend or foe if they should encounter another in the field. This was to be only in a desperate situation where vital information critical to the operation was to be shared out of necessity, such as suffering a mortal wound.

Designated areas of safe retreat or safe houses would be available and known and used only by the clan as alpha cells. Alpha cells would provide many required resources, such as money, weapons, travel papers to any country in the world. In remote areas beyond civilization within 50 clicks, there was food provided.

Cleaners designated as Omega cells comprised wet crews skilled in cleanup and restoration after a firefight, leaving no trace behind as though nothing unusual had ever happened.

There were many recruits that filled much of the lower tier stations in the Nightshade organization. The special recruits possessing psychic talents were few, but certainly favored above the rest. Their skill set allowed secret access to otherwise impossible places and conditions. Using their second sight, as it was called, worked like an advanced form of remote viewing, serving as a momentary peek into future events and to provide advanced intel for other team members.Recruitment was constant, but they always gave priority to those involved in the recruiting process to seek the special ones that showed promise.

It was not until the fall of 2006 that a special emergency meeting was called by the CGA. This time, they held the meeting at the penthouse floor of the plaza hotel in New York city.

It was a brisk sunny morning. A cool wind gusted intermittently, making any scarf around the neck inadequate. Only a few senior council members arrived in attendance. The members ushered themselves quickly from the black limo into the warmer hotel lobby by single file. They passed the concierge station and headed straight for the penthouse VIP elevator with grim determination. The formal meeting began with the chairperson wrapping his knuckles lightly on the conference room table. The chairperson inquired of the liaison from the remote site designated the 'hen house', if any new recruits showed promising development.

The Vice chair leaned forward. He expressed delight as to the prospects of a recent recruit, one who is recovering from a road attack in Iraq. He lies in a coma in one of many secret hospital triages. Continuing further, that those overseeing his recovery assured him. He is in an induced coma, but may promise greater skill than one other, code named Scorpion.

The chairperson leaned back in his chair, obscuring his face in the shadows. His facial expressions slightly revealed by the sporadic but dim light of his cigar.

"So, tell me, the chairperson inquired nervously, who is this new champion arriving on the scene?"

The Vice chair continued. "His true name is Graywolf, an Apache from the San Carlos reservation in Arizona. He enlisted along with others from his tribe, but all died except our candidate in a road bomb incident in Iraq."

"Graywolf came through the ranger program with colors and further showed excellent independent leadership ability, along with courage and bravery under fire, which are well established. Graywolf is now undergoing intense paranormal training and expected to awaken early next Spring and ready to hit the field running."

The chairperson smiled with a grunt. "Next spring, huh?" He tossed ash from his cigar into a nearby ashtray as he grunted another remark. "Too bad he won't be ready until then. Keep me posted on this one."

The Vice chair nodded in the affirmative. "Will do!"

Again, the familiar surroundings of the cavern dissolved. Graywolf found himself within a small clearing near a forest of tall pines. The sound of Osceola's voice seemed to echo from above, beckoning him to enter the forest.

He called out toward the sound of the voice while following a narrow path partially obscured by a thick layer of leaves. In his early childhood, he would hide his movements with a tree branch, spreading leaves randomly behind his tracks from those who were trying to find him during hide and seek games. He struggled to navigate the under-brush and unexpected rolling terrane. The light shining through the branches above from the warm morning sun illuminated his way.

"I can hear you, but I cannot see you." Graywolf declared, hoping to bolster his confidence on the rightness of his direction.

Then the voice sounded loud and close by. Graywolf stopped, turned and found Osceola standing behind him, smiling.

"You appear to know where you are going, young warrior! But can we well use your confidence?"

Graywolf's expression of confidence fade quickly. He sat down on a small outcropping. Osceola looked down at him, still smiling.

"Oh, you've decided now to take a rest when your journey has only just begun!" Osceola declared.

At that moment, the light of the sun vanished. The blackness of the dark enveloped him. The path he had traveled was no longer clear. Now there were only vague shadows of trees surrounding him. Then Osceola's tone changed.

"In this forest are many mysteries. This forest is also teaming with animal life, such as that rather large grizzly bear approaching from the south. He looks starving! I believe he has already caught your scent. So, for your sake, I suggest you make a run for it… now!"

Graywolf jumped to his feet, with his heart pounding out of his chest. The quickness of his pace, driven by the imagined demise of that damn bear, making a tasty meal of his body. He quickly realized that he could not see all the many obstacles in his path forward. The underbrush and unseen fallen tree limbs easily navigated in the light of day, now strewn randomly and perniciously before him.

They purposely tripped him, causing him to stumble often. As he increased his pace briefly, thereafter, followed sudden unexpected drops in the terrane slowing him down as he tumbled again to the ground. The distance between him and the roaring sound of that bear's paws pushing nearer through the brush, grunting and growling in hot pursuit.

Then Osceola's voice whispered calmly to him.

"Now you can realize you cannot rely on your eyes in this situation. You must go inside and embrace the forest with your heart. Let your heart guide you past the obstacles in your path. It is your mind that tries to rule over you. You must get hold of your fear and stop it from clouding the stronger connection to the forest that is only possible with your heart-mind."

"The day is for those who are blind, weak and vulnerable. The night will be your best and only ally. You must come to trust it more. So, feel the support of the forest by allowing it to change your actions. Intuitively sense its quiet and affirmative guidance. It is not your enemy, so make it your friend. Your life depends on it," Osceola said with a warning.

"Lean into the darkness as you would embrace a lover. Get hold of the fear that hovers over your heart, shrouding your inner vision from view. Let it become instead the razor's edge of your inner vision, clearing the way before you. It will make your movement precise and flow more naturally."

Graywolf wanted to make the most of his movement, especially far and away from the grimace of that bear moving ever closer. He stopped briefly to catch his breath. His fear kept his chest from expanding to take on fresh air. He bent over and grabbed his knees, taking that precious moment to gather his mind and his feelings. He realized he could not outrun the beast, but he thought elevation might be his only advantage. As he ran again, his focus was more on the trees standing nearby rather than those lying down as obstacles in his path. He remembered from his childhood his father's warning. Bears can climb as well as run. To escape the snarling monster closing the gap between them, he ruled out his father's words. He would pick a medium to small pine, which the bear might not care to attempt.

He moved to climb quickly to the upper branches of a pine nearby, where it grew flimsy. The sap ran rich on the bark high above, making his grip slip more easily. The bear arrived frustrated and roared into the dark sky above.

Graywolf watched below as the bear circled his tree. Then the grizzly stood up on his haunches and grasped the tree trunk, shaking it vigorously as one might try to dislodge an apple clinging to a branch. The tree swayed with broader movements. Graywolf felt the shudder of his heart with every swipe the bear made. He was worried. He looked about to see if there was another tree nearby. The closest pine he estimated to be at least a ten-foot from him. The urgency pressed him to consider the impossible. There was no doubt he would need to cross.

Instead of waiting for the bear to break the tree into a stump, he synchronized the bear's swipe with a corresponding push with his weight to move the upper trunk toward the desirable pine nearby. He needed just one more push, but then the bear leaned into the trunk and snapped the trunk into toothpicks. The tree fell, but not in the most helpful direction. He placed his feet against the trunk, expecting to leap at a moment's notice.

The momentum of his jump toward the adjacent trunk caused that tree to break as well. Now, Graywolf and the new tree headed for the ground, near to the angered grizzly. The tree he desperately clung to just moments before held out the only possibility of safety. Now that cherished pine was falling near an unseen cliff nearby. The upper trunk reached out beyond the overhanging cliff, leaving him dangling above the ravine far below.

His left arm wrapped tightly around the trunk while he scrambled to find something to grasp onto below the cliff with his free hand. He knew his time was short. Meanwhile, the bear approached above, snuffling and grunting with displeasure. The bear sensed his presence and rolled the felled tree, hoping to reveal his prey. Graywolf hung on tightly as the trunk rolled back and forth, helping to loosen his grip.

He stared wide-eyed at the undergrowth below the cliff. He spotted a few small roots exposed from the underbrush above. His only chance now was to let go of the tree trunk. His best and only chance was to lunge toward the cliff wall. Then he felt the tree topple over the cliff and he jumped with all his strength to reach the exposed roots.

He landed a little below his proposed target, the roots. Graywolf found his grip entrenched in mostly loose soil, which gave way from the outcropping above. He lunged again and again until his fingers reached the smaller branches of roots. As he kept reaching for a better grip, he watched the trunk topple over the cliff past him. He tried to see through the darkness below, but it was mostly black, covered by a slight gray mist.

After some eternal moments passed, the felled tree landed on the rocks below with a loud snapping and crunching sound. Graywolf closed his eyes for a moment in thankfulness that it wasn't his body and bones snapping on the rocks.

The bear relinquished his pursuit. He meandered

away, giving off a few whimpers of disappointment. His salivating drooled between his sharp teeth and one other tooth that had broken off many years before. Disappointed that his lunch had just escaped his hungry pursuit.

Graywolf struggled to bring the rest of his weary body back onto the upper cliff surface. A hand suddenly thrusted out to offer help. It was Osceola. As Graywolf pulled himself up and onto safe ground, he laid on his back, releasing a deep sigh of relief, but still panting from his near-death experience. As he looked up, Osceola's friendly expression beamed a broad smile upon him.

Then Osceola said.

"It's a terrible thing to live in fear, isn't it? Fear cannot harm you, it is just a feeling, like hunger, anger or frustration. This is where your mindfulness training will be very helpful. This lesson you have learned well. You kept your head and used your intuition and insight to override your fear of impending death. You outmaneuvered the monster and avoided your certain demise. So, we shall move on to your next phase. We will begin your mindfulness training next."

The view of the cave returned a sweet sense of maternal safety. Osceola did not hesitate. He continued with the introduction to the mysterious components of his mind.

"Young warrior, he began, there are three distinct compartments that make up the core of your capacity to think and reason. Unfortunately for you, you have been using, or should I say misusing, your levels of mind haphazardly. It is not your fault really because you lacked the proper training from your youth, which makes all of your movements erratic and even chaotic."

Graywolf rebuked Osceola's comments.

"I survived the bear attack, did I not?" Graywolf declared in his defense.

Osceola continued without acknowledging Graywolf's defense.

"Obviously, a certain quality of good fortune hangs on you, my young warrior!"

Graywolf felt his confidence waning again.

"But teacher, if I had failed, would I have died by being devoured by the beast, or crushed on the rocks in the ravine below?"

Osceola answered. He turned his back toward Graywolf. Then he gave an answer. "Though your training ground would seem to offer you invaluable experience without the punitive effects of your failures, your mind would have completed your demise because those circumstances would have given your mind no other alternative but to accept the logical outcome, the unfortunate end to your life."

Graywolf's feeling of vulnerability gave rise to an increase in emotional stress. Osceola sensed his response and added. "Young Padawan, your sense of your near-death experience continues to plague you. You will need to let go of that continued lethargy. You only need to consider, while in your meditations, your obvious mistakes. Then discover how to correct them for the future. But you must not waste your energy considering what might have been. Alternative realities do not support forward movement, only when and if they offer positive solutions to your perception of your present circumstances."

"There are actually three different levels of mind. The first level, which is the most obvious to you, is the so-called conscious mind. This level of consciousness is not actually conscious most of the time. You are not aware and connected to the true reality of existence. They smothered this level in delusion and fantasy and it is ignorant of the programming you have received since your birth. That programming is part of your daily experience, and even you contribute to it. Your task is to discover the nature of your programming and how you respond to it."

Graywolf looked bewildered by Osceola's comments.

"Teacher, if I am driven by these unconscious programs, how will I be able to step back and understand their nature and influence? It seems impossible!"

Osceola continued.

"It is true what you say. That is the reason the vast majority of people go through their lives blind and deaf to their correct actions, feelings, and the reality of independent thought. That is why you need to understand the impact and reality of the two remaining levels of mind."

"The second level relates to what they often refer to as the subconscious mind. Your subconscious is much more aware of the true reality. Because of your programming, it is unavailable to you, which has become your silent bodyguard. It protects you from harm, such as emotional trauma. It is a brilliant organizer of all of your forgotten and fragmented experiences throughout all the days of your life and even continues to conduct a cleanup program while you slumber of unfinished mental business of any sort."

"Perhaps it is the most powerful of your mental makeup, because it handles the reality you experience when you are supposedly wide awake. It is scanning you every moment of every hour in your day, trying to determine what is the most important issue that troubles you and makes it a priority. It will either block your awareness of those troubling issues, or it will change your outer experience to accommodate a more tranquil and peaceful solution to the disturbance. This actually makes you more vulnerable in the pseudo-reality you live in."

"Timid to interrupt Osceola, Graywolf begged to ask. So, is it the master and I am the slave? How can it create the reality I am experiencing? Does that not describe a hopeless existence with no chance of escape, a dream for which I can never awake?"

Osceola smiled.

"Now that is exactly what I am getting at. The great Spirit told me you were a quick study! Normally, that would be the case. In your situation, you are to become an instrument of the light, and they have given me a task of awakening your mind to the truth of this universal reality."

"I connected your subconscious mind to the vast network of energy ribbons that bind the universe together. You could say that the universe is one giant mind that governs all sentient beings and their subsequent evolution. It beseeches the subconscious to bond with the conscious level in order to work more harmoniously with change. The problem is that the universal mind keeps knocking at the door of your subconscious expecting a response. As the universal mind reaches out to the subconscious to welcome it into the universal fold, the subconscious is so burdened with internal and external programs it cannot respond. These programs act like a thick jungle overgrowth that prevents easy access for the universal mind to bring about your natural evolution."

Again, Graywolf interrupted Osceola's diatribe.

"Teacher, is this universal mind, God?"

Osceola responded.

"This supreme awareness is much like water. It can fill a cup. Though one could say that the cup defines the water's shape, if then the water pours out, the cup remains as a cup, a mere vessel to hold the water. What of the water then, where does it go, and does it change as it enters other vessels or other substances? No! The water remains constant, even when it combines with other substances. Even if the container breaks, it does not adversely affect the water. It simply escapes the broken container, seeking another form that is more accommodating. So, part of your training will encompass the idea that form is not permanent, but quite malleable.

Whereas, the energy of the supreme awareness is constant and permeates the entire universe."

"The third level of mind is crude and underdeveloped, more like a beast. As it governs the instinctual consciousness, it is dangerous when allowed unbridled freedom. It is the hindbrain, relating to the most primitive reptilian aspect. It considers survival as supreme and will, if pressed, fight to the death to overcome any obstacle, including competition within its own species. First to emerge in man as an animal among animals. An evolutionary and unpredictable creature always frightened at the unseen and unknown and predominantly violent. This sort of consciousness fits well with the world of old, a primitive world filled with predators and prey. Avoiding skirmishes and conflicts if possible, only to live another day facing starvation or obliteration at every turn."

"It is said that the human became self-aware when all three levels of mind emerged. But many outside factors were to play an important role in the man's evolution-creature. Man cannot develop into a higher form unless these three aspects of the mind are in harmony and work together. Only then will the outer reality begin to change and represent more accurately what grows within."

"In the meantime, you will need to focus on rebalancing those three elements. The first is the predominantly conscious mind. The fervent intellectual that believes in nothing but itself is the bully of your consciousness. It attempts to reconcile the unknown with denial and disbelief, or worse, substitution. It tries to suppress the subconscious with potent feelings; feelings of guilt, anger, jealousy, fear. These energies distract and work to keep the other parts in line.

Remember, the heart mind is supreme and must have oversight of the others. It has the last say. So, too much of your struggle will be between these two."

"The subconscious is literal. There is not much analysis, and it is less philosophical and does not interpret on its own. It can, when it chooses, accept straightforward commands. It is direct and blunt, with no sense of diplomacy or protocol. Being aligned with the hindbrain, it will yield to fear and threat with an equal and use of violence to defend itself to the death."

"The subconscious is in direct connection to the quantum field and, if need be, can influence the quantum of reality with surprising results. Those results would convince anyone else you were nothing less than superhuman in your abilities. This is so because you will appear to alter the fundamental axioms or laws of physics known in the quantum reality of the physical. You will experience more of these abilities in your Nagual training."

Graywolf had unknowingly passed out during Osceola's training. When he awoke, he felt embarrassed and wanted to plead guilty to his misdemeanor, then apologize. Osceola was gone! Graywolf's plan to make amends crashed hard on the floor of the cavern. He worried he had angered Osceola with his lack of focus. Graywolf wanted to complain about his tiredness. He believed it was a sign of weakness. This feeling emerged out of his tribal experience. Graywolf called out to Osceola, but he didn't respond.

Graywolf left the chamber and explored other areas of the cavern, but no sign of Osceola. He felt abandoned and sat upon a broken stalagmite nearby. He wanted to plan a new plan and search the cave for a way out when a small gust of wind rushed in behind him, enticing him to look around. To his relief, Osceola was standing quietly just a few feet away. Graywolf's concern dropped as he let out a quiet sigh. He was relieved to see his teacher again.

Osceola smiled at him.

Graywolf exclaimed. "I went looking for you. When I could not find you, I wondered if I had imagined you all this time."

Osceola's smile broadened. "Are you in a rush to leave? Where did you think you were going? You cannot leave because you haven't finished your training yet! I will let you know when it is time for you to go from this place, and since I alone hold the keys to your exit, your leaving is not an option. Besides, is not your choice to end the training. You have barely touched the surface of what you need to know."

Graywolf tried to apologize, hoping to neutralize his master's displeasure with him. Osceola brought his hand up to stop Graywolf from talking. His tone became soft and reassuring.

"Your concern is unwarranted. You simply fell asleep, so we let you rest for a while. Interesting that you should bring up your imagination along with your doubt. That will be our next focus with your training, the right use of your inner and outer will as it pertains to the use of your imagination."

"First, there are two kinds of will; the inner will and the outer will. The inner will come from your solar plexus, while the outer will come from between your shoulder blades just below the nape of your neck."

"Most humans relate the will as a kind of power of mind, applied to attempt control of an outcome of situations you are not fond of, or downright dislike such as, procrastinating from actions you need to take mitigated by masking it with hesitation or reluctance to personal changes you need to make. This form of will needs to be relegated only to the element of mind control."

"Inner will shall provide the true power to effect change to unfold in life. It doesn't require the mind at all. Your emotional state spawned it, perhaps what you would call a determination to succeed with your aspirations. We will develop a stronger emotional center in your work. In your case, that will be key to the purpose of your being here, to learn and master the elements that control the supernatural."

"But I thought emotions need to be controlled to create greater balance, which can avoid the dangerous situations that appear when the emotions are uncontrolled. As an Apache, my grandfather taught this and his father as well. So, you are saying this is not a valid way to be?" Graywolf declared with astonishment.

Osceola continued.

"It is true, but only from a certain point of view. Your tribal way is to use your mind to suppress your emotions. Not only is this an aberrant way to handle your emotions, but it also robs you of your vital power to act appropriately. This is the wrong use of outer will and makes your spiritual movement awkward.

"Your mind needs to be brought in to guide your powerful emotions, not suppress them. Here is where the inner will can be of greater benefit in all ways." Osceola confirmed.

Graywolf then inquired. "How do I reach my inner will? My father and grandfather only spoke of the gut courage one needs to be a great warrior."

Osceola added. "Yes. Courage is one of the greater forms of inner will. But it is an emotional feeling current that springs out of the solar plexus, or gut, as you call it. Out of that same place can bring forth other significant aspects of will, such as intuition, clairvoyance and clairaudience. These aspects give you a glimpse into the future and provide additional information you will need to navigate the Nagual. In the semi-conscious human, this is called a hunch."

Graywolf pressed Osceola further. "Master, what is the Nagual?"

Osceola smiled slightly and continued.

"Good question, young warrior. The untrained consciousness can not see or experience all that is the Nagual. The vast majority of humans ignore any apparent existence in this part of reality. They are mere robots going about their lives unconscious of the vast and greater reality of the quantum, what the watchers call the Nagual."

"Where is the Nagual?" Graywolf continued.

Osceola smiled a little again.

"The Nagual is all around you. It penetrates and surrounds you wherever you may go. It completely supports the conscious man with his destiny. Your destiny is now to complete your training so that the Nagual will become your closest ally. It will provide you with the insights and energy to allow you to be an effective tool for the light."

"It functions with your feelings and your inner will and will readily respond to you as you apply your developed skills. It also responds to the power of sound."

This astonished Graywolf, then asked. "You mean I can actually talk to it?"

Osceola responded.

"Well, yes, but not in the way you think. The sounds of power are not your words spoken in the languages you know. These are special sounds that only enlightened beings can utter. These sounds have a kind of alphabet containing 52 verbal sounds and 20 sounds that are silent."

Puzzled by Osceola's description of silent sounds, he continued to pursue this strange comment. "How can a sound be silent? That idea seems contrary to me!" Graywolf declared.

Osceola continued to explain.

"To make a sound that is silent requires a special application of secret knowledge about the structure of your body and its unique capability to utter these special sounds. They do not come from your vocal chords that you used to form the sounds of words. They come from an unused portion of the voice box called the Malthuk organ. In antiquity, it has another name which is very difficult to pronounce. So, we have given it a name that you can more easily relate to."

"When you say the sounds that are verbal, they contain several overtones that will resonate through the ventricles in your brain, resonating harmonically, allowing the sounds to bridge the gap between the physical world you know and the unseen world of the Nagual. When you speak silently, the overtones that are made, you cannot hear except for the consonants that may emerge above a whisper."

"The name of this spiritual language is called Vrill. It is identical to the angelic speak offered to those fortunate enough to have had contact with beings on a higher level, all of which is part of the Nagual. You will learn to develop this organ and we will teach you how to speak with it."

Graywolf bowed his head and exclaimed.

"Master, I was a terrible student with language usage. I failed most of the courses I took in elementary school. Apache came naturally, but English I learned to speak from my Shichoo, or grandfather. It took many years and only then I could barely write what I spoke."

Then Graywolf chuckled.

"My Shichoo would complain that a pidgeon could speak and write better than me!"

Osceola ignored Graywolf's perception of his lack of lingual ability.
He declared crisply.

"Do not judge your past attempts at communications. These are very different lingual skills and do not require you to write these sounds down because they do not hold a visible meaning to anyone except those beings and the energy that pervades in the Nagual."

"The verbal Vrill is spoken with a combination of vowels and consonants. We grouped them into two, three and four-letter syllables, depending on the need and the goal desired. These become formulas, which can bring about changes in your physical location, surroundings and actions that unbelievers would describe as the use of magick."

Graywolf said sheepishly.

"So, am I to become a sorcerer, brujo, or a shaman as my tribe originally wanted me to become?"

Osceola frowned at this remark.

"No, my young warrior. You will become an enlightened warrior with skills given upon your efforts that have been the strongest desires of many want to be sorcerers over the many centuries. Attrition lost much of the ancient knowledge regarding these skills, either through deliberate actions or simply dissolved. Either through deliberate actions or simply dissolved. The watchers have obscured the truth."

The term watchers caught Graywolf's attention.

"Master, who are these watchers you have referred to?"

"These are entities that have overseen the world and its development over eons of earth time. They are beings of renown, beings of light that maintain the Nagual and seek to preserve it from abuse or misuse, the guardians of the gate of knowledge and power. They will eventually take over my task with you and will become your confidants, guides, and teachers in the ultimate completion of your destiny."

Graywolf was sitting on his favorite stalagmite, practicing his deep breathing techniques given by Osceola. Then he felt that familiar rush of air behind himand realized his master was nearby.

"Hello master." Graywolf uttered quietly, only with his breath.

Osceola smiled and answered him in his mind.

"Your skills of perception are improving, young warrior. Your telepathic ability is also improving as well. That is good! So, from now on, I will speak to you only in your mind. This is important because with your shape shifting work, you cannot speak the words you rely on. It will be your mental communications that become of paramount importance. This is true especially with the watchers, as they only communicate this way."

Osceola continued.

"The most important thing to remember when speaking telepathically is to remember to pause after you've spoken. The tendency of all students of the occult is to rush ahcad speaking and not allow the important hearing a response. It is not entirely your fault, for it is your cultural experience to want to be the center of attention governing the space with an incessantly busy mind! You would be rude if you did not allow an exchange of conversation, yes? This acknowledgment is especially an important protocol when addressing the watchers. To them, it is a sign of your training, of course reflecting on me, your teacher. But it is a demonstration of your respect for the higher intelligences that will rule over you in my absence."

Graywolf could hear his master's voice as clearly as if he had spoken aloud. He found a certain reluctance to speak in this way. He felt concern for speaking out of turn or worse, not making any sense while working with his mind.

At first, Graywolf over compensated in his efforts and didn't realize his intention became a kind of mental shouting. Osceola stopped him.

"Graywolf, you don't have to shout your thoughts. We can hear you easily from galaxies far from this place and with only a whisper. You can speak softly and not fear your thoughts would not carry the distance. In the Nagual, your thoughts and feelings are the main chattel of exchange. Your thoughts and feelings will directly power your actions of change and movement. Therefore, we focus more on this part of your training. With vague thoughts and worse, vague feelings, it is, as you might describe, mixed feelings. Verbal language allowed these,with little or no effect, but will only result in unwanted outcomes in the Nagual."

"Your first lesson in Vrill will be two syllable expressions. We will begin with those Vrill that pertain to internal windows of energy we call lupahs. There are seven lupahs inside your being. These are, mostly, active, but not balanced properly."

"As a point of interest, Apache language is near to Vrill. One reason they chose you to be a shaman of your tribe is because the elders saw you were an apt pupil and even your previous shaman recognized your innate skills and chose you to replace him."

"Now we want you to focus in the groin's region, somewhere near the spot between your anus and your genitals. From there, breathe deeply, as we have shown you. Utter the two-syllable sound of BM. We pronounce this with the lips parted. Not spoken with your vocal chords, but uttered deeper in the throat passage as 'Beh Meh.' This utterance will allow for greater energy and force to come more easily unto your base, or pelvic region. It will strengthen you. Even ten regular men could not overpower you once you have mastered this Lupah."

"Practice this for the rest of your day. Then we will speak more about the difference in speaking to the Nagual and extending that vibration into the physical world as you have known it."

Graywolf felt exhausted after his practice and fell asleep on the cavern floor. He awoke to find the sound of his master's Vrill summoning him to wakefulness.

"Now young warrior, let us add to your new vocabulary with the utterance of LM, pronounced as Leh Meh, also uttered deep within the voice cavity of the throat. This is in tandem with your conscious mind focused on the region of your navel. It handles your ability to reach and manipulate the elements to your inner will. As a shaman, calling upon the elements to do your bidding in the physical realm, known to many great shamans. When mastered, you will control fire, water, earth, and air at this level when mastered. Now spend the rest of your day to practice this, Vrill."

Graywolf nodded with acceptance. Again, exhausted, he sat against the stalagmite and fell asleep sitting up. This time, however, his sleep, disturbed by a strange grumbling in his stomach, often followed by the excessive belching of air along with many waves of nausea.

When his master's vrill entered his mind, he smiled and responded.

"Hello master. I'm ready and awake for your next lesson."

Osceola smiled.

"That is good, my young warrior. Enthusiasm and an eagerness to learn are very important character qualities needed in the work of transformation. So once more, we give you another set of Vrill syllables geared to release more energy in the solar plexus area. This time it is RM. Pronounced as Rch Meh at the deeper part of your throat. It connects your belly brain to the solar logos, intelligence that lives through the portal of the sun.

Contrary to scientific opinion, the sun is not hot but a portal to higher dimensions."

Graywolf was stunned by Osceola's words. He could hardly believe such an outrageous idea! He suddenly felt awkward. Then he quickly reached deep inside his soul for some kind of composure, something his grandfather taught him if he faced a questionable adversary. His grandfather had intended it to be for a white eye, but Osceola was not a white eye, but a brother.

Graywolf tried to make light of Osceola's comment.

"You are joking about the sun, yes?" He said nervously.

Osceola paused for a moment before answering telepathically.

"Does that news disturb you? This is not new! Perhaps, at some point later, you may find the truth regarding the solar orb radiating the earth with the light and warmth. The untruth is so easily accepted by many at its face value."

"Listen, young warrior. There will be many shocking and difficult concepts presented to you.

Your re-education is already underway and will continue to be quite provocative. However difficult this may be for you now, you soon discover that all of what you learn, from me and later from the watchers, is all quite true. Your understanding will soon expand to embrace the impossible."

"Now we continue. The next level is at the heart. The Vrill syllables for that lupah are HW or He Wa. I will continue with the last three lupahs sufficient for this evening's practice. At the throat is a more advanced Vrill. It contains three syllables; ERM. This pronounced as EE-RehMeh."

Graywolf interrupted.

"Master, why does the throat have three syllables?"

Osceola answered again.

"The throat lupah controls two energetic actions. First, the energy of expression and second, the energy of reception. Two of the sounds control the two actions independently, while the third sound balances their oppositions into harmony."

Graywolf said nothing but nodded in a sign of understanding.

Osceola continued.

"The next lupah is at the brow. Its syllables are also three, SRM. These are pronounced as Shi Reh Meh. This lupah determines what you see before you in the physical realm. Also, it presents what you don't normally see, which lies in the Nagual. Finally, the last lupah is at the top of your head with another three syllables, ARO, pronounced as Ah-Reh-Ooh. This lupah determines your connection to the watchers and to the noble spirit."

"Practice these in the sequence as I have given. In a week, we will see how you are progressing. Now the hour is late and you must rest. You can continue with your practice after a small amount of refreshment in the morning."

The hours passed with Graywolf's mind swimming amid the Vrill he learned, revolving around him like a carousel of animals, squawking the sounds at him mockingly. As the last animal appeared, it was a raven. The bird seemed larger than life, and his fiery eyes glared at him, suggesting a subtle nuance of familiarity. It cawed at him several times and then the bird's sounds merged into a screech of Ah-Reh-Ooh as it flew up and out of sight. Then he opened his eyes. Standing before him was Osceola looking down at him with a slight grin.

"Good morning, young warrior. I trust you slept well?" He said telepathically with an innocent tone.

"Dreaming in the Nagual has significant benefits. Time becomes like a butterfly. It alights from moment to moment, touching the reality of the world, but does not have a reasonable arrangement of logic.You believe it to be the next morning. Your mind tells you logically that you remember the previous evening's discussion, which was then followed by a long nap. So logically, it would seem to be the next day. Ah, but alas, like the white eye's Rip Van winkle legend, you have been practicing your Vrill for almost a year while you lay here dreaming!"

Graywolf's expression suddenly changed to one of horror and disbelief. As he struggled to put physical words together, his mouth became dry. Only air came out of his mouth instead of audible words.

Osceola looked on sympathetically.

"Perhaps you need to quench that fire of dryness with a bit of refreshment!"

Osceola handed him a small cup. The liquid looked blue, and the cup was distinctly warm to the touch, inviting him to sip from it slowly. It smelled of peppermint, but then changed to the sweetness and spiciness of nutmeg.

Meanwhile, in the cubical that Graywolf's body lay, an attending nurse came to his bedside to arrange his bed clothes when she noticed he seemed to choke and then a blue fluid appeared at his lips and dribbled down his chin. The nurse ran quickly to get the physician in charge of the ward. When the doctor appeared, he scanned Graywolf's body and took a handkerchief from his lab coat and wiped the fluid away. He smiled at the nurse and declared.

"Not to worry, lieutenant. This sort of thing can happen in these cases. He is still in a deep coma. After all these years, it's not likely that he will come out of it."

The nurse gave a small sigh of disappointment

and nodded with acceptance.

Graywolf smiled after drinking the blue fluid. He felt refreshed and energized.

"What was in that drink, anyway? It was very unusual, but tasty."

Osceola smiled and responded.

"We have our ways to support and further the work. We cannot give you solid food at this point. Later, we can accommodate your physical needs differently, but for now, the fluid intake will suffice."

"Your skills with Vrill are on par with the next phase of your training. As a spiritual warrior, you will need an additional component in your training to support your future efforts of fighting crime in the world."

"The world has become corrupt. Even at the highest levels, the darkness has infiltrated many judicial offices that would otherwise forward the cause of justice. The focused attention is on rectifying these crimes against humanity. These organized attempts at lawlessness are now unbounded. Large criminal groups have coalesced to operate systematically and cooperate beyond the law."

"This requires a different approach that also operates beyond the law. We seek now to find our own unbounded ways to deal with such lawlessness. That is where you come in. After your training is complete, you will join and take an active part in this good fight. There are others, your colleagues already in the field, with similar skills. They welcome your graduation from this training. They will work with you in tandem to accomplish a common goal, an effective system to fight against these criminal forces where they live and operate. Re-establish the balance of power between the light and the dark in the world."

Graywolf stared at the floor of the cavern and then looked up at Osceola.

"Ok then, let's get it on. I'm eager to add my efforts to the cause."

Osceola grinned and added. "So be it!"

Osceola's tone changed in that moment.

"We have chosen a power animal for you we believe offers the greatest freedom in your actions and a perfect and stealthy way to mingle without drawing attention to yourself. Your animal form will be the Raven."

"As you have learned how to control fire, air, water and the earth, now you will learn the Vrill that builds a greater and more intimate relationship with the elemental aspect of the Nagual. In short, your native tribe would describe this as shape shifting. It is not only the Vrill that can accomplish this, but you will need to learn how to merge your consciousness with that of the raven's mind."

"All species function through a group mind. Normally, in the physical world different species live side by side separately. You will become a traveler in two worlds, the physical reality and the Nagual reality. You will need to shift into the Nagual reality at will, by your own volition. I will give you the Vrill that will begin the process."

"Beh Che Reh Ah Vau Eh Neh becomes your calling card, so to speak. You will now use this expression in your practice. I will now instill into your consciousness the Raven Mind consciousness. You will focus your attention and use your inner will to merge with the Raven Mind."

"At first, this aspect of your training will strike

you as weird and certainly different, perhaps emotionally strange. Your mind will not process in the same way as your human mind processes."

Graywolf pondered this and then asked.

"So, will I need to agree to the Raven mind and its way? Will I still keep my human mind?"

Osceola responded.

"Yes. You will direct your Raven consciousness, but then you will need to allow the raven's consciousness to function freely as well."

"The concept that your form can assume a different shape is not only foreign to most people, it falls into the narrative that this is an impossible action and a fantasy, not a fact of reality. That disbelief becomes the foundation of your cloak of your protection. Your true identity is a secret and known only to your benefactors."

Graywolf suddenly inquired.

"So, who are these mysterious benefactors you speak of?"

Osceola considered Graywolf's question. Having previously deliberated whether to tell Graywolf once he awoke was now shelved. Osceola decided it was time he came to understand who he would work with and for.

"We know them as Nightshade. Your government is not part of it. They have been operating behind the scenes in the world, making sure that the powers of darkness which try to invest in the actions of criminal elements to further their goals, do not exceed the balance of power between the light and the dark forces on earth."

"The criminal elements around the world were unorganized. As long as these elements sought only to rule over small regional territories, it was not a significant concern. The forces of light believed that local law enforcement could handle these problem areas by themselves without interference."

"When powerful and wealthy crime barons were now organizing to coalesce all the independent clan factions into one global alliance, their activities showed an unusual and sweeping rise in political corruption with a common goal for world dominance."

"This powerful and well-funded group of criminals showed an unusual and more powerful allegiance to something beyond the usual human activities of greed and violence. The forces of light discovered that dark shadow forces intent on swaying the political and military forces of key nations were actually behind this insidious plan."

"Rather than risking an all-out confrontation with this dark alliance publicly, they felt this action would create confusion, chaos and mayhem and greater harm to innocent people. The forces of light created and guide a new secret alliance among an independent group of dedicated and wealthy members of the business community, also having important political connections."

"They wanted to build a small army of special warriors endowed with certain supernatural abilities. These warriors could then effectively fight these dark forces secretly as vigilantes, authorized to function effectively outside the limited laws of the land."

Graywolf's reaction was solemn. He gritted his teeth, remembering the loss of his friends. After the road bomb unexpectedly exploded in Iraq, killing all but himself, his guilt of survival confused and overwhelmed him. He lost his will to fight and just wanted to die with the respect. Sad he did not sacrifice his life along-side his friends. He wept from the loss of his comrades in Iraq. Graywolf, still sobbing, apologized to Osceola for his weakness.

Osceola looked on and commented.

"Young warrior, we need not embarrass you with your feelings for your friends. They knew the risks of dying in battle, even though they had not even had the chance to actually engage. Yet, even now, they are looking on with great anticipation of your continued efforts to fight the good fight."

"They feel you can do what they could not do. You will make up for the indignation they suffered while offering their good wishes for your success."

Upon hearing Osceola's words and encouragement softened his pain. His will and determination renewed now with a higher spiritual purpose. He felt more aligned with his Apache heritage with a promise to avenge the meaningless deaths of all of his friends.

Osceola's tone changed.

"Let us continue with this next phase of your training. I want you to call upon the mental image and the consciousness of the raven mind. With that present, then utter the Vrill I have given you. You must muster your inner will along with your feelings focused to merge with the raven, as you would merge with the loss of your friends in battle. Only then will your transformation begin."

Graywolf let his mind relax. He reached inside for the images and consciousness of the raven's mind. As he delved deeply into the raven's consciousness, he could faintly hear the cry of the raven. With each push to engage, the cry became louder. Each cry then came closer. He suddenly realized that the cry was now actually coming from inside his throat. Instead of words of amazement, there was just a cawing! Spontaneously, he raised his arms out beyond his normal reach. He could hear the ruffling of feathers. As he waved his arms furiously, he suddenly became smaller and lighter. With a wondrous lunge, his movement and thoughts arose.

To his utter amazement, he sat high above a much

taller stalagmite. His view was strange and tunnel-like. When he looked down upon Osceola, smiling with praise, he realized he had no feet and only talons gripping the tall stone which had become his perch. His transformation was complete. He was now a raven.

Two Colonels arrived at the military triage holding Graywolf. Their rank and identification provided passage past all the security checkpoints until they reached Graywolf's room. No one questioned their presence.

They stood quietly at the foot of his gurney, looking down on Graywolf with some expectation. Then the first agent said in a whisper.

"He is still sleeping. What do we do now?"

The second agent responded also in a whisper.

"Don't worry. He will awaken soon. Let us prepare the way for his evacuation from this place."

Then the second agent placed his hand over Graywolf's head and uttered Vrill. Graywolf's body twitched a little and then stopped, following a deep breath.

Then the first agent turned to the second agent and said.

"Did you give him the rendezvous coordinates?"

The second agent simply responded with a nod as they exited through a rear stairwell of the building. Once outside the rear exit, they both dissolved into a wisp of gray fog.

Moments later, Graywolf awoke, feeling disoriented. He looked around and realized he was in some sort of clinic or hospital. He looked down to find an IV in his arm. Then he turned to the soldier lying on a gurney next to him, still in a coma. Quickly, he switched his life support connections over to him to not arouse attention. He had little time. He could hear talking outside his room. Sliding out of his bedcovers, he crouched down low enough to see through the door's window but dared not to be seen. His heart was pounding out of his chest, blocking any clear thoughts. He shook his head violently back, trying to get his head straight from the sedative they had just given him. Graywolf struggled to shake it off. His vision faded and blurred, but he waited to see if the doctors and nurse would leave. They turned to walk further away and around a corner. He saw his chance to break away and took it. He slipped through the door and went down the same stairwell the agents had taken. Upon reaching the outside, the light was blinding. Hearing two armed military guards approaching, he quickly sought refuge behind a garbage bin until they passed.

He wanted to transform into his animal form, but being drugged could not accomplish that. Graywolf doubted that the total experience was only a figment of his dreaming while in the coma. He sought to escape with a military vehicle that was parked nearby, praying the driver left the keys in the ignition.

He slipped quietly into the vehicle, keeping low to the floor until he found the precious keys. The keys were not in the ignition, so he feverishly checked the glove compartment. Still no keys! Then he checked the seat and the floor behind. No keys there either, body now upended while feeling around on the floor. Reaching under the seat brought nothing. The illusive keys were not to be found.

He was about to give up when something sharp poked against his shoulder. Wanting to yell from the pain now raging against his shoulder, he merely whispered the shout of pain while gritting his teeth. Then the pain brought his mind into focus and he realized it was the bloody keys poking at him unmercifully.

He raised the keys into the lock carefully while he comforted his wounded shoulder. His hand shook badly, as though he had suffered from Parkinson's.

He thought, if only he could reach the gate, there would be only one guard at that post. That was his best chance to get off the base and mingle with the local traffic.

They still dressed him in his bedclothes, so no chance he could fool the guards. Then he sat mortified when the two guards returned and passed right in front of his vehicle. They looked at him and stiffened, following with a smart salute from both.

This shocked Graywolf! Then he looked down to see he was in dress fatigues.

He looked into the rear mirror to see he was wearing a major insignia on his shirt lapel. He could not fathom how this was possible, but he wasted no time running with this charade.

He offered a meager return salute and shifted the vehicle into drive, driving with agonizing slowness until he reached the gate. He held his breath when the guard emerged from the gatehouse only to salute him again, commenting with a smile, "have a nice day Major."

Graywolf returned his smile with a nod. He was off the base and on the main street leading into town. Fearing his mysterious disguise would soon fade into exposing him to further trouble. He suddenly felt an urge to turn onto the main highway, leaving the village. This puzzled him , for he did not know where he was going. The road he was on felt 'right' somehow, so he continued on until it was almost dark. Up ahead was a small dirt road leading off into a meadow, with many trees forming an excellent hiding place. Until he could break through the drugs coursing through his veins, he would be more or less useless. After exiting the vehicle, he suddenly felt exhausted. He placed a few branches over the vehicle and chose the foot of one of the nearby trees perched high on the hill. The tree gave him the high ground, offering him a good lookout and temporary solitude and sleep. He thought to himself.

"Strange. I should feel tired, since who knows how long I have been sleeping in that hospital? I'll bet I have had enough sleep to last a lifetime!"

Hours later, Graywolf awoke, startled to see two persons stand over him. Alarmed that they had found him and were prepared to take him back, he attempted to scramble unsuccessfully to his feet. The two strangers were not from the base.

The first agent stooped down at eye level.

"Well soldier, your head must be screaming in pain about now. The sedative they have given you is one of their strongest. No Matter. It will wear off in time."

The second agent extended a helping hand to Graywolf. Once on his feet, he still weaved a bit. He asked them in a shaky voice.

"Who are you? Where am I and what is happening?"

The first agent replied.

"No worries, mate." He retorted with a distinct Australian accent.

"Now be a splendid fellow and come along with us, so we can get you to a safe house and briefed properly."

Graywolf was desperate for some meaningful

answers.

"Where are you taking me? How did I get into these clothes, anyway?"

The second agent responded kindly.

"Actually, you are still in your bedclothes. We afforded you a proper cloak so you could leave that place with no serious difficulty."

At that moment Graywolf looked down and found he was in fact still dressed in his bedclothes, which bewildered him.

"But how did you do that? Are you some kind of magician?"

The agent went on.

"We have similar skills that you have. We have mastered the art of masking our true appearance from ordinary people. You might say that it is a kind of mass hypnosis. You have this knowledge as well, but you still need to practice what you have learned. Try to contain yourself until we get to the safe house. I will answer all of your questions in due time, I assure you."

After traveling for more than an hour, their vehicle pulled into a driveway leading to an old abandoned farmhouse.

The first agent turned to Graywolf.

"Okay sport. This is as far as we go, but it is the last stop for you. Just go right into the house. The team is waiting for you." The agent said, while gesturing for Graywolf to exit their vehicle. Graywolf turned to see the agents leaving him and he continued to inquire after them.

"But who are you people? What am I doing out here in the middle of nowhere?"

The agent's voice trailed off to Graywolf. "Go inside, my boy. You will learn all you need to know from the team."

The vehicle was already some distance from him and cloaked by exhaust and dust. Graywolf still called after them, exclaiming. "What team?"

Graywolf approached the farmhouse front door cautiously. As he reached for the door handle, the door opened by itself. He hesitated to enter until a friendly voice beckoned for him to enter.

Inside were several strangers standing around, as if they were waiting for something to happen. Then, in that moment, a bright flash of light cast shadows behind everyone present. As the light subsided, a figure loomed into view, it was Osceola.

Graywolf let down his defenses only enough to feel the shock of seeing his dream teacher actually standing before him. Frozen, he could not speak or move. He could hear low murmurings coming from the group. It sounded familiar. His thoughts coalesced to realize it was Vrill he hearing. They were chanting together the same sounds. Fear re-emerged, clinching against his heart.

Just as Graywolf felt the urge to run away from this very odd assembly, they stopped and Osceola turned to Graywolf and said.

"Come now, young warrior, we are among friends, especially after so years of working together! You need not consider running away. Besides, where will you go? The family you are thinking of is gone. You died long ago, as far as they are concerned. They moved on! If you seek them out, it will only frighten them and reintroduce greater pain and horror for them to reconcile your presence."

Graywolf finally broke down the frozen vocal chords he knew were still intact.

"Master, what is going on? Who are these people and how is it possible you can actually be physically and standing here? Are you not of the spirit?"

Osceola began slowly.
"Well, yes, and no. I can be present in your mind and then I can also be manifest. It is very difficult to maintain this form for long."

"So, for now, I will be brief. You are being introduced to some of your fellow shadow warriors. These warriors will be your field training team, building your skills to move between the physical world and the Nagual easily and gracefully."

Graywolf felt a twinge of fear mixed with a longing for the safety of the cavern.

"Master, will I see you again?"

Osceola looked at him with a glimmer of

sympathy. Then he went on.

"As a bird turned out of the nest into the world from the safety of its egg, so it is with you, now reborn and now re-enters the world not as a man but more than a man. You will learn to make your own way, as a Nagual man, to navigate the harsh reality of the space in between the multi-verse."

In that moment, Graywolf saw Osceola dissolve into a mist. The room was silent. Graywolf turned away for only a moment. Then, as the vapor cleared the room, he could feel all eyes focused directly on him. He wanted to end that irritating feeling, like a lab rat being observed and perhaps judged for the expected behavior.

One of the team stepped forward, speaking with a heavy English accent.

"All right then, let's get on with it ole boy! Uh… Graywolf was it? Well, for a start, I believe you are a contradiction in terms. By that I mean, you come to us as Graywolf, yet you are training as a Raven. It seems strange and perhaps even perverse! However, as you will soon learn, those who map our behavior are supremely intelligent and rely heavily on our abilities to reconcile applying their plans in the physical realm while we work to adjust the circumstances to make sure that their plans unfold."

Graywolf turned to face the Nagual agent and glared, saying.

"I admit I may be green with all this, but for what it's worth, I have been studying this magic for who knows how many years! So, how about we do some kind of equality across the board, mutual respect but not based on experience?"

The Nagual agent drew a slightly wry grin.

"Well gentlemen, I believe we have the makings of a good sport here, and duly noted my friend and soon to be colleague. At that moment, he thrust out his hand in a gesture of friendship.

Graywolf expected further rebuke or humiliation, but to his utter surprise, just the opposite happened, an easily recognition granted.

Cautiously, Graywolf reciprocated with a firm grip. The agent, encouraged by Graywolf's return gesture, reached past his hand, grasping his forearm, locking their arms intimately together, as warriors traditionally do when greeting trusted friends and comrades in arms.

The group of Nagual agents crowded around Graywolf giving him emotional support for what he will now face, a series of trials all geared to develop his skills, but importantly that his skills and confidence must be acute and with an ability to expedite his transformations with quickness and agility.

The first of his trials makes up a kind of Nagual obstacle course. The English agent pointed Graywolf to the door, exclaiming what he must do.

"Okay, my fine feathered friend. Remember, your wolf's side may keep your wits about you, but this is about relying more on the raven qualities you possess. You will need to think like a raven, and behave as a raven would. So, when you encounter an obstacle, call upon the raven mind."

"Once outside, head for the barn in the back. That is the gateway to the path you will proceed on. We will time you on this course. So, do not dally or wait, keep moving no matter what you might encounter."

To Graywolf, it sounded more ominous than the

obstacles Osceola had placed in his path. This was different. He was awake now and not dreaming! He felt this was different. Real physical consequences lie ahead if he faltered or otherwise miscalculated his newfound abilities to meet the challenge presented to him.

The click of a stopwatch proceeded a command to "Go"! Graywolf darted out the door, sprinting to the rear, aiming straight for the barn. Just as he was about to reach for the barn door, an invisible wall abruptly halted him. He stopped long enough to find out the wall was surrounding the whole barn. Any normal approach was beyond circumvention.

He reached out with his heart, focusing on the raven's mind. Suddenly, he got the impression: *cannot go through, must go over.* He closed his eyes and stretched out his arms. With his knees bent in a crouching fashion, he lunged forward, imagining how he would fly over the barn. Moments after, he found himself perched on the roof vent, peering down at the area behind the barn. He swooped down to the ground only to find they caught him in a net. His struggle to get free brought no result as a raven. Then he thought of his body. In a flash, his claws became hands ripping and tearing open the net, freeing him. He immediately jumped to his feet and sprinted into the woods. He looked down to see he was naked. That was an unexpected result. Another impression seared his mind: no distractions!

He quickly cast that thought aside and continued to run barefoot. Then he felt sharp pains in his feet and, upon looking down with a certain horror, he realized he was landing on shards of broken bottles. They were everywhere! He could not stop running though because standing on broken bottles was worse than running over them. He imagined the lightness of his body and raised his arms, once again reaching for the air to support his movement. Soon after, he was glad to see his wings carrying his bleeding feet over the path of broken bottles to a clearing ahead.

When he reached the clearing, he relaxed his attention as the raven and once again assumed his human form.

Relaxing was not a suitable stance to take, for

soon he realized he was being pursued by a medium-sized cat bent on having him as his next meal. Graywolf yielded for a moment to his human instinct and tried to outrun his predator, offering only meager attempts to avoid his nemesis as a prey animal.

Twice the cat took swipes at his legs, hoping to bring down his prey quickly. Thus, confirming the much-anticipated meal was soon to come. Graywolf's legs were badly bleeding from the attacks. His human thoughts brought concern for losing blood and possibly weakening, but he vowed to keep running. Then the raven mind again interjected a brief and solemn warning: Fly now, not a moment to lose.

He felt some odd resistance rising. No change was occurring! He realized, he locked into his human form. Panic entered his heart, imagining the cat having his way with him.

What was wrong? He thought. Just as the cat made a last lunge to take him down, Graywolf remembered it was not his mind that determined his form, but his heart was key. He felt the raven mind trying to help him and he felt such gratitude he burst into his raven form, narrowly escaping the cat's last attempt.

He was suddenly soaring above the cat in a circle, peering down at the predator with a sigh of relief, but his sigh became a series of caws as he broke the circle and flew away. He flapped his wings vigorously to speed up his speeding safely away.

Beyond the clearing there was a dense underbrush of thicket full of thorns. He entered the thicket, fully expecting his feline predator to pursue. In moments, the cat was upon him, standing just outside of the thicket growling and swiping at the thorns, trying to clear a path to Graywolf. Every swipe brought blood and pain to the cat. Soon the cat felt this prey was not worth his effort and sauntered away in frustration.
Graywolf flittered through the thorny underbrush, convinced the cat had given up his pursuit. Once out of the thicket, he resumed his human form.

As he limped forward toward another small clearing, he did not lose his attention this time. When the Nagual agents appeared before him, he leaped backward. The agents smiled and said.

"Relax, my friend. You are not in any imminent danger at the moment."

"Well, you were a few minutes behind the normal time allotted to this obstacle course, but you did well to augment your circumstances with an appropriate response in each case. So, we will consider this, your first trial, a success."

Graywolf would continue his trials after he recovered from his wounds.

His timing was always a little off. In time, his skills improved and confidence with his new abilities was paramount.

The Nagual agents continued with his martial training, teaching him shortcuts with his movements, enhancing his speed and agility. Even as he worked to spar with the agents in teams of two and three at a time, he learned to augment his martial attacks and defense with his shape shifting.

One evening the team and Graywolf sat around a fire, drinking some warm concoction that fortified and sped up battle injuries. Then, in a flash of light, Osceola appeared before them.

He first addressed the team inquiring of Graywolf's progress.

"So, gentlemen, is he ready?"

They all resounded in a common refrain.

"Yes, master, we think he is ready for his first solo encounter.

Osceola looked pleased and turned to Graywolf.

"So, my young warrior. You have done well. Your training team has approved your passage to the next step. So be it! Now it is time for you to engage with the enemy."

The next morning, Graywolf made an early flight to Madrid. They briefed him that two agents would meet him at the airport with a code word response.

Upon landing at Barajas International, he brought along one small piece of luggage. Once past the gate and into the main arrivals area, he searched for any sign of agents. No one approached him. Near a window looking upon other planes arriving, he found a seat. He slurped on a semi-warm cup of coffee, hoping to quicken the grogginess from the long flight.

A stranger sat next to him. Graywolf attempted to say something to him, but he hesitated. The loudspeaker suddenly interrupted his silence and announced.

"The incoming flight from Lisbon is now delayed. Please come to the ticket counter for seat assignments on another flight."

The stranger than got up to approach the counter. He felt relieved. He made the right choice to keep silent. Feeling bored, he wondered around. Various duty-free shops allowed him to pass the time. Graywolf grew concerned. No one approached him yet. He felt anxious and wanted to leave the secured area.

He noticed travel postcards nearby. He gazed at the photos of New York and other major cities. One card displayed the city of Chicago. He had never been to Chicago. The next card was from New Mexico. Behind that card, a picture of Tucson brought a sadness to his heart. He clenched that card tightly, lamenting about the Res. He wondered, was his father and other members of the tribe still alive? His thoughts got interrupted. A man's voice sounded behind him.

"Nice place Chicago. I visited there once, but didn't like the wind. Personally, I prefer the southwest. You ever been to Arizona?"

Graywolf considered the question. Then realized the code word within the sentence. His response was simple.

"No. Arizona is too hot for me!" That was the response phrase.

"Maybe I will go there someday." He added.

He turned to the man standing behind him. They shook hands as the Nagual agent smiled at him.

"Welcome to Madrid. I have a car waiting. Shall we go?"

Graywolf nodded in the affirmative. As the car transported them to the safe house, two agents briefed Graywolf on the mission in Madrid. The first agent, Jerome, explained his job would be a simple. Intelligence revealed that WMD's (weapons of mass destruction) arrived a few days before, on a tanker bound for Brazil. However, intel has not discovered the location of the stolen material.

"Officially, the second agent, Phillipe, said. We know from Interpol, a brokered deal to dump the waste material would occur here in Madrid. Our agents in Stockholm intercepted a coded message on the dark web. Talking between high-ranking members of the Hezbollah revealed the plan to sell to the highest bidders invited to Madrid."

"We believe the suppliers and product came from Iran through Syria. The weapons comprise several drums of spent Cesium 137 powder. This material is very toxic. Along with a conventional delivery system poses a serious threat to an already unstable

Middle East."

"Our reliable sources have analyzed this plot. There will be many devices made with this dirty core applied to a standard plastic explosive and distributed to key cities set to go off simultaneously. The unexpected chaos will cause shifting the blame to the Israelis, controvertibly, the Israelis will blame the Muslim terrorists in Iran and Syria."

Jerome continued.

"Their goal is to derail the UN Security Council's vote to provide sanctions against certain Muslim block nations guilty of human rights violations and the support of terrorists.Certain Zarqawi cells moved in to fulfill this larger, more ambitious plan. They want to destroy the peace initiative, halt the sanctions and free their comrades in prison."

"In addition, Phillipe added. Talks between coalition leaders of right-wing conservatives and the leftwing radicals have broken down, blaming each for the roadblocks to peace. Jihadists are pushing for greater visibility and more effective violence in the area. Our group has already quietly eliminated another competing group seeking to steal the WMDs from the Zarqawi factions. That would only make this operation more difficult."

Jerome then went on.

"We interceded, creating an opportunity through back channels of the United Emirates to purchase the waste material on behalf of a fake cell of jihadists."

"That exchange will occur tonight. As an observer, you are part of the backup support. If anything should go awry, shift into your animal spirit, and observe only from above and out of sight. You may not take action unless absolutely warranted. You understand?"

Graywolf nodded to confirm.

Then Phillipe confirmed.

"They set the meeting for 6pm. The location is at an abandoned garage on the south side of the city. Here is a copy of an aerial reconnaissance photo taken of the building. Note the 'X marks its location' in the photo. You need to memorize it and burn the photo afterward." Again, Graywolf nodded. "The safe house is near to the garage. You will have a little time to prepare yourself at the safe house after we drop you off. Don't be late! In fact, as a raven, you can even arrive early. You will become a forward sentinel, reporting back anything out of the ordinary."

The car pulled up next to an unusually high curb, a common earmark in the outskirts of Madrid. Graywolf struggled to exit the vehicle, trying to avoid the curb. He stood for a moment, watching the car speed away. Then he turned to face a narrow three-story building wedged between two storefronts. One store sold a variety of goods with a stand of vegetables in front. The other store was a humidor, offering a variety of smoking instruments and attire, along with brass oil lamps.

The three-story building presented a broken sign clinging to a shutter hanging above the entrance. The sign identified the building as a hotel. Only the name 'The Blue Parrot Bar-cafe' was clear. They obscured the sign defining the lodging part, leaving only a handwritten message in Spanish. Rooms were available!

Graywolf entered the small, tattered lobby. The proprietor sat in a small anti-room hunched over his desk reading a paper. He puffed casually on a foul-smelling cigar, rivaled only by the smell of the proprietor's clothes. He wreaked of cheap cologne and stale body odor. His unshaven look revealed a balding scalp. A few remaining strands of greasy hair plastered down, with several beads of sweat threatening to drop freely from his brow. He looked up and smiled, shifting his cigar to one side to speak.

There was no shame or regret that his smile revealed several missing teeth. Yet, one gold tooth leaned outward prominently to help give dignity to the spaces left behind by his other missing teeth. Several paths of tracks of human traffic on the dusty floor showed a sharp lack of tidiness all around. Graywolf guessed they had not swept it in months.

Graywolf reluctantly offered a friendly greeting.

"You have a room for me. The name is Nantan Lupan?"

The proprietor looked at his ledger. He spun it around for Graywolf's signature. Before Graywolf finished signing, the proprietor shoved a key toward him, exclaiming.

"Your room number is 3A. It's on the third floor at the top of the stairs. They paid you up for the night. If you want to stay longer, you must pay in advance, and that will be cash."

Graywolf gave a nod to accept his terms. Slinging his backpack over his shoulder, he climbed the stairs. The first board creaked, a not-so-subtle warning of the state of the staircase. As he bounded to the first landing, the proprietor yelled out.

"Mind that fourth step on the second staircase. It's a little weaker than the rest!"

The third floor was even more dust laden than the ground floor. He thought.

'Well, my stay will not be long, fortunately!'

Graywolf pushed the old key into the lock, but needed a jiggle for the lock to open. The door appeared less secure than he wanted. He closed the door behind him, peering through several holes prominently displayed.

There was one window in his room with one window pane missing, allowing some outside air to enter. He mused to himself. 'Ah, I am afforded natural air conditioning with no additional cost!'

He dropped his backpack onto the mattress and sat down. His body weight pressed the few remaining springs close to the floor. 'Hmmm… He thought. Won't be sleeping much here, I suspect.'

He looked at his watch, marking the time, and said to himself.

"Okay. It's 3:15pm now. I have about two hours before I need to transform."

He went into the cramped bathroom and glanced into the tub area. He hesitated to weigh in on a shower. Noting the unsanitary conditions of the tub, he changed that idea and resigned to just washing up in the small sink. He turned the faucet on at the sink. Only air came out. Then after, it sputtered some dark foul liquid.

Giving up on anyway to clean up, he went over to the window, casting a gaze upon the adjacent rooftop below. It had rained recently. A large puddle of water gathered at a sloping corner of the roof. Though the window is now nailed shut, the missing pane of glass offered fair egress. No good for a man, but certainly for a raven.

He sat down in a well-worn chair made of

wicker. His body and mind slipped into darkness and deep sleep. Two hours passed. His eyes opened to see the room was now dark, illuminated only by the streetlights below. Leaping from the chair, his heart pounded. He glanced nervously at his watch, scared he might have missed his appointed rendezvous. He sighed with relief. There was still plenty of time.

He stored his backpack under the bed out of plain view and began his Vrill chant. Reaching up and out with his arms, he crouched into a lunging position. As soon as he connected with the raven mind, his vision narrowed into a circular halo around his line of sight. His body suddenly became lighter. An ache between his shoulders returned as his black wings carried him aloft to the missing window pane.

He spied the pool of water below and darted down to splash himself vigorously. When satisfied he had shaken all the dust from his feathers, he leapt into the air. Off he went, soaring and flapping alternately, bringing him high above all the buildings, then swooping down around street signs and trees. He wanted to further hone his skills at flying in his new form.

He thought to himself. "Hmmm… Traveling as the 'crow flies' has definite advantages. It's quiet up here, beyond any traffic concerns. He never considered being a bird, but it was fun and soon it felt like second nature!"

Soon, his target was in sight. Soaring in ever tightening circles until he found a suitable perch. Along the ridge of the roof, a series of air vents provided openings for him to enter unnoticed.

Once inside, he sat on an overhead crane, giving him an ample view of the comings and goings below. Three sedans pulled into the garage, one after the other.

A fourth vehicle arrived containing his new agent friends. The man at the entrance stared inquisitively at their vehicle. It came built less for style and more for an all-terrain travel experience. The door man waved them on as he closed the door behind them. The key buyers exited the vehicles only after their guardian soldiers toting automatic weapons took their places ahead of their leaders.

The buyers approached a long table in the middle of the room. The group selling the weapon material stood behind the table along with their guardian protectors standing alongside, also armed with automatic weapons. Talking was low and difficult to hear. Graywolf noted the atmosphere was tense. All seemed civil for the moment.

Then the tone suddenly changed. The sellers declared with a loud voice that they discovered treachery. The deal would not go down until they reveal the real identities of those betrayers. Turning their weapons on the agents, the agents knew their cover was now known.

Jerome immediately dropped into his power animal, like a large leopard. Many moved away while his partner, Phillipe, shifted to becoming a deadly cobra. One soldier took aim at Jerome. Just then, Phillipe the cobra lunged at the soldier, sinking his sharp fangs into the soldier's neck. Then the dynamic duo attempted a coordinated effort of offense between martial attacks in combination with their animal counterparts. They effectively assaulted their attackers while defending each other.

Jerome the leopard swiped his sharp claws against one seller's leg while twisting wildly and biting through one of the seller's forearms, ripping it from his elbow joint. Before he could bring his opponent down, they shot him in the head and killed him. As Jerome's body fell to the floor, the garage space then filled with automatic weapon fire from all sides.

Phillipe struck two other gunmen before a large cleaver from behind severed from his body his head.

Gun fire continued as Graywolf swooped down from the safety of his crane perch. He flapped about the group, catching the defending soldiers off guard. With the power of his momentum, and the element of surprise, he increased his speed, heading straight for the faces of the gunmen. He clawed wildly in each case, tearing at their eyes, ripping them from their sockets. Several blinded gunmen dropped to the floor dropped their weapons screaming. Graywolf used that opportunity to change back. He rolled on the floor, sweeping up their guns and sprayed a hail of bullets in their direction to finish what the opponents started.

In the aftermath, the room displayed lifeless bodies strewn everywhere. He knelt down next to the remains of his colleagues. He placed his fingers across the carotid artery of Jerome to confirm his demise. Poor Phillipe's condition was more obvious. His body now slumped below the table, missing a head.

Graywolf stood frightened, feeling alone and lost. The remaining members of the selling party made their escape during the mayhem. It was a total disaster. They got nothing for their trouble and they still needed to find the missing Cesium powder. Memories of his road bomb experience rolled back upon him and that all too familiar sense of helplessness and frustration returned.

Transforming back into his raven form full of sadness and despair, he felt a longing to go home. He flapped his wings hard, pushing ever upward through and beyond the rooftop with anger. He wanted desperately to push away the old sadness together with the burden of the new sadness. Rising high above the city, not flying now with joy but with terror and loneliness. Graywolf flapped and soared into the clouds, screaming out his 'caw, caw, caw,' high above. He drank in all the silence afforded to him. He sought solace, but only the darkness of night surrounded him, offering him little comfort in the heavens above.

A severe storm unexpectedly developed from the southwest while Graywolf was still aloft. His flight now became labored and harsh. The horror of the garage scene continued to weigh heavily on his consciousness. He worried that his transformation would turn back to a human form before he could land. His struggle against the high winds increased. He could not keep his mind clear. His emotional reactions over the loss of his newfound friend/agents and the deaths he caused disturbed him. The question returned and again. "What happened at the garage? What went wrong? Nothing made sense!"

Flying now seemed less fun and more utilitarian, but flying against strong winds definitely sucked! He was ready to return to the safety of that dusty old hotel room.

When he finally landed on the ledge of the open window, he was glad to get back. He hopped through and flittered to the floor with his human form already unfolding to completion. For a moment, he could not feel his legs. He thought.

"Oh my God, I hope I have transformed, okay?

He lay on the floor for moments, trying to sense if his transformation went badly. He raised his head for a better view, but they bent the major portion of his legs around the bed frame. That old worn chair sufficiently blocked any descent view of the transformation process. It did not occur to him they had turned the chair over, all the bed covers ripped away from the mattress while the mattress, also gutted by a knife.

Scanning under the bed revealed his backpack's location changed. Now it lay under the mattress, tangled in the bedding, escaping the rampage of someone's search. He sat up to take stock of the violent intrusion of his space. Then he felt a presence. He was not alone! An undefined figure stood in the room's corner.

The identity of the stranger eluded his scan, well cloaked by the darkness. He jumped to his feet, crouching in a defensive posture, prepared to ward off another attack, considering transformation again, but that was out of the question because he could not muster the energy or enthusiasm to change. He resolved himself to a human battle if necessary.

Much to his surprise, the stranger turned out to be no other than Osceola.

Osceola spoke to Graywolf in a soothing manner.

"Well, my young warrior. You have had quite an introduction to the life of a shape-shifting soldier. Certainly more than we expected. For your first time in the active arena of intrigue and danger, clear and present, I am happy that you handled yourself well, and you survived! Even better, your timing and choice of the use of your power animal was excellent."

Graywolf interrupted his master.

"Master, I could not save Jerome or Phillipe. I feel I failed to provide adequate backup support for my colleagues. It reminded me of being, once again, the only survivor of the battle just as before."

Osceola continued.

"I know how you must feel. You realize that the two circumstances are completely different. You must not blame yourself in either case. If you had moved in more quickly, you too would have suffered from your demise! No, my young warrior, you did well. You lived to fight again for another day.

"Come now. There is a car waiting outside of the hotel. I have arranged for one of our drivers to take you to the airport. You will find in your bag first-class tickets to Paris, connecting them to London, where you will meet other members of the second team. Your code phrase is: "It is always springtime in Paris." Your response will be: "Yes, until it rains.""

"We believe some unknown factor betrayed our agents. One assailant carried a tattoo on his neck. The tattoo appears to be the web of a spider. Our team is coordinating an investigation of that symbol with our sources at Interpol. In the meantime, let us get you back to a friendly space so you can tend to some of your wounds and get some much-needed rest. This battle is not over, my friend. It has just begun. The challenge appears much larger in scope than we first believed. I will contact you after you arrive in London. Be well, young warrior.""

Osceola dissolved into a mist. Then Graywolf immediatelyput on a fresh shirtChapter 20.Questions of Allegiance.

A severe storm unexpectedly developed from the southwest while Graywolf was still aloft. His flight now became labored and harsh. The horror of the garage scene continued to weigh heavily on his consciousness. He worried that his transformation would turn back to a human form before he could land. His struggle against the high winds increased. He could not keep his mind clear. His emotional reactions over the loss of his new-found friend/agents and the deaths he caused disturbed him. The question returned again and again.

"What happened at the garage, what went wrong? Nothing made sense!"

Flying now seemed less fun and more utilitarian, but flying against strong winds definitely sucked! He was ready to return to the safety of that dusty old hotel room.

When he finally landed on the ledge of the open window, he was glad to get back. He hopped through and flittered to the floor with his human form already unfolding to completion. For a moment, he could not feel his legs. He thought. "Oh my God, I hope I have transformed okay?

He lay on the floor for moments trying to sense if his transformation went badly. He raised his head for a better view, but the major portion of his legs were bent around the bed frame. That old worn chair sufficiently blocked any descent view of the transformation process. It did not occur to him that the chair had been turned over, all of the bed covers ripped away from the mattress while the mattress had also been gutted by a knife.

Scanning under the bed revealed his backpack location changed. Now it lay under the mattress tangled in the bedding, escaping the rampage of someone's search. He sat up to take stock of the violent intrusion of his space. Then he felt a presence. He was not alone! An undefined figure stood in the corner of the room.

The identity of the stranger eluded his scan, well cloaked by the darkness. He jumped to his feet crouching in a defensive posture, prepared to ward off another attack. He paused to consider transforming again, but that was out of the question because he could not muster the energy or enthusiasm to change. He resolved himself to a human battle if necessary.

Much to his surprise, the stranger turned out to be no other than Osceola.

Osceola spoke to Graywolf in a soft and soothing manner.

"Well, my young warrior. You have had quite an introduction to the life of a shape-shifting soldier. Certainly more, than we anticipated. For your first time in the active arena of intrigue and danger clear and present, I am happy to see that you handled yourself well and moreover, you survived! Even better, your timing and choice of the use of your power animal was excellent."

Graywolf interrupted his master.

"Master, I could not save Jerome or Phillipe. I feel I failed to provide adequatebackup support for my colleagues. It reminded me of being, once again, the only survivor of the battle just as before."

Osceola continued.

"I know how you must feel. You must realize that the two circumstances are completely different. You must not blame yourself in either case. If you had moved in more quickly, you too would have suffered from your demise! No, my young warrior, you did well. You lived to fight again for another day.

"Come now. There is a car waiting outside of the hotel. I have arranged for one of our drivers to take you to the airport. You will find in your bag first class tickets to Paris, connecting then to London, where you will meet other members of the second team. Your code phrase is: "It is always springtime in Paris." Your response will be: "Yes, until it rains."

"We have reason to believe our agents were betrayed by some unknown factor. One of the assailants carried a tattoo on his neck. The tattoo appears to be the web of a spider. Our team is coordinating an investigation of that symbol with our sources at Interpol. In the meantime, let us get you back to a friendly space so you can tend to some of your wounds and get some much-needed rest. This battle is not over my friend. It has just begun. The challenge appears much larger in scope than we first believed. I will contact you after you arrive in London. Be well young warrior"

Osceola dissolved into a mist. Then Graywolf immediately put on a different shirt slinging his jacket and backpack over his shoulder, closing the door behind him.

On his way out of the lobby, he detoured toward the hotel manager's office. shoving the room key toward him, Graywolf commented snidely.

"Your room was exceptional, but I didn't care much for the view!"

The hotel manager sneered at him making a face and promptly offered his forearm in a thrusting up motion as in a grand physical obscenity.

As Osceola had promised, a car was sitting in front of the hotel, engine running.
As Graywolf got in he added.

"Barajas airport please."

The driver nodded. The headlights swung around past the hotel as the sedan headed out of the square, speeding its way into the night. Graywolf leaned back into the seat, as the sedan drove by the area where the garage shooting occurred.

The police stationed patrol cars everywhere. The entire area and street was blocked and barricaded. All vehicles coming in or going out were being checked.

The sedan slowed to a halt as the police officers approached asking for papers and inquiring to the driver about his passenger. They wanted to know his business and destination.

The driver turned to ask for Graywolf's passport. He handed it over reluctantly. The driver collected his own and added it to Graywolf's, then handed them to the officer. After shuffling the documents around, the officer gazed intermittently into the sedan, aided by his flash light. He attempted to compare photos with the passenger. Fortunately, the officer was not inclined to arrest anyone in the moment. Then the officer returned the documents back to the driver and motioned for them to move on.

Graywolf stared out of the rear window as they pulled away from the scene. He watched as the rain falling on the window formed streams that flowed in front of his view. All of the lights from the patrol cars flashed multiple colors mixing together in a rainy kaleidoscopic fantasy. The view to the outside forced him to reflect inside on the day and evening experiences.

He wondered about the training, the wisdom of

Osceola, the other agentsthat helped him develop his new skills and those agents he saw die, even though they possessed shape-shifting skills, the skills did not save them! Then he began to questioned his abilities to shape-shift. He felt doubt that he would survive another encounter. Then he considered the ethical approach of his recruitment. This all began when he was in a coma. When did they ask him to join their band of warriors? When did he agree to do this? He could not answer those questions.

He realized, he does not actually know who these people are! Is he really working for the light, or is this some weird and twisted scheme to use his skills to eliminate competitors within the crime syndicate? Graywolf's confusion and guilt tangled with his anger.He felt too tired to offer any further resistance to his involvement in this magical maniacal scheme. The dazzling display of lights finally lulled him into a deep sleep.

It was morning when the sedan pulled in front of the airport entrance. The driver turned to awaken Graywolf. Several attempts by the driver finally aroused him to open his eyes. He sat up and looked about.

"Are we here?" He said sleepily.

The driver responded.

"Yes. We just arrived. If you hurry, you can still catch your flight to Paris. It leaves in half an hour. You have your tickets, so go straight away to the boarding area."

Graywolf grabbed his backpack, momentarily checking for his tickets, then exited the sedan raising his hand to gesture a 'thank you' to the driver. As the sedan pulled away, he added in a shout.

"Thanks for the ride."

He paused to readjust his pack on his shoulder more securely. Then he began a sprint through the crowds as if he were on another obstacle course. The trick was to navigate the people while minding the signs above leading to his departure gate.

The stewardess walked to the gate exit and began to close the door when Graywolf approached out of breath.

"Wait! He cried. I have my ticket right here. He waved the ticket wildly in the air like a refugee might wave a white flag. Then he pleaded.

"Please. I need to make this flight."

The stewardess stared at him for a moment. She smiled politely and accepted his ticket. As he entered the gangway he could hear her announce.

"One more passenger is boarding late for Flight 194 to Paris." Slinging his jacket and backpack over his shoulder, he closed the door behind him.

On his way out of the lobby, he detoured toward the hotel manager's office. Shoving the room key toward him, Graywolf commented snidely.

"Your room was exceptional, but I cared little for the view!"

The hotel manager sneered at him, making a face and promptly offered his forearm in a thrusting up motion as in a grand physical obscenity.

As Osceola had promised, a car was sitting in front of the hotel, engine running.
As Graywolf got in, he added.

"Barajas airport please."

The driver nodded. The headlights swung around past the hotel as the sedan headed out of the square, speeding its way into the night.

Graywolf leaned back into the seat, as the sedan drove by the area where the garage shooting occurred.

The police stationed patrol cars everywhere. The entire area and street were blocked and barricaded. All vehicles coming in or going out were being checked.

The sedan slowed to a halt as the police officers approached, asking for papers and inquiring to the driver about his passenger. They wanted to know his business and destination.

The driver turned to ask for Graywolf's passport. He handed it over reluctantly. The driver collected his own and added it to Graywolf's, then handed them to the officer. After shuffling the documents around, the officer gazed intermittently into the sedan, aided by his flashlight. He attempted to compare photos with the passenger. Fortunately, the officer declined to arrest anyone at the moment. Then the officer returned the documents back to the driver and motioned for them to move on.

Graywolf stared out of the rear window as they pulled away from the scene. He watched as the rain falling on the window formed streams that flowed in front of his view. All the lights from the patrol cars flashed multiple colors, mixing in a rainy, kaleidoscopic fantasy. The view to the outside forced him to reflect inside on the day and evening experiences.

He wondered about the training, the wisdom of Osceola, the other agents that helped him develop his new skills and those agents he saw die. Even though they possessed shape-shifting skills, the skills did not save them! Then he questioned his abilities to shape-shift. He felt doubt that he would survive another encounter. Then he considered the ethical approach of his recruitment. This all began when he was in a coma. When did they ask him to join their band of warriors? When did he agree to do this? He could not answer those questions.

He realized he does not actually know who these people are! Is he really working for the light, or is this some weird and twisted scheme to use his skills to eliminate competitors within the crime syndicate? Graywolf's confusion and guilt tangled with his anger. He felt too tired to offer any further

resistance to his involvement in this magical, maniacal scheme. The dazzling display of lights finally
lulled him into a deep sleep.

It was morning when the sedan pulled in front of
the airport entrance. The driver turned to awaken
Graywolf. Several attempts by the driver finally
aroused him to open his eyes. He sat up and looked
about.

"Are we here?" He said sleepily.

The driver responded.

"Yes. We just arrived. If you hurry, you can still
catch your flight to Paris. It leaves in half an hour.
You have your tickets, so go straight away to the
boarding area."

Graywolf grabbed his backpack, momentarily
checking for his tickets, then exited the sedan,
raising his hand to gesture a 'thank you' to the
driver. As the sedan pulled away, he added in a shout.

"Thanks for the ride."

He readjusted his pack on his shoulder more
securely. Then he began a sprint through the crowds
as if he were on another obstacle course. The trick
was to navigate the people while minding the signs

above leading to his departure gate.

The flight attendant walked to the gate exit and closed the door when Graywolf approached, out of breath.

"Wait! He cried. I have my ticket right here." He waved the ticket wildly in the air like a refugee might wave a white flag. Then he pleaded.

"Please. I need to make this flight."

The flight attendant stared at him for a moment. She smiled politely and accepted his ticket. As he entered the gangway, he could hear her announce.

"One more passenger is boarding late for Flight 194 to Paris.

Meanwhile, another criminal despot arises from the mainland of China. His name is Doctor Fu Lau Chu. This Chinese Syndicate leader rules from an unidentified island located somewhere in the South China Seas.

His businesses cover the usual; exporting drugs such as opium and cocaine, prostitution and human sex trafficking and money laundering and extortion And protection racketeering. Though he operates through Beijing as his main distribution point, he lives mostly on his island called Nemesis.

Doctor Chu has summoned his captains to discuss his plans for expansion into the west. This would not be a peaceful transition. Many factions will more than likely resist his invasion of their turf. However, Chu is undaunted by this expected resistance. Confident with his plan, an intense focus which has been underway for many years, is a slow and deliberate undermining of alliances within the other clans.

He is both relentless in his endeavors. His reputation precedes him. Not unlike the Muslim cells of the near and middle eastern bloc countries, he modeled his organization around the mythical Hydra, a dragon of many heads. He chose the symbol of a spider's web encompassing the seven-headed dragon at the center. He insists that all of those dedicated to serving him have a brand on the neck with his symbol of power.

Doctor Chu arranged for his captains to meet him at the King's Joy restaurant in Hong Kong. To ensure privacy and security, he rented the entire facility, including the adjacent hotel for rooms, for one night.

Doctor Chu began his meeting with a rousing lecture of his intent to dominate the world's leading criminal organizations.

"Our approach is intimidation, through the clandestine and systematic elimination of those who are the leaders of those other clans." He stated.

"The first steps will be by my finest assassins. We well trained them to function much like the ninjas of feudal Japan. They will infiltrate their defenses, create chaos, and then murder their leaders. This will make it easier for us to recruit from their ranks."

"Also, we want to cease working through other intermediaries. We need to seize the production and distribution of our cocaine and opium products out of the hands of such ignorant pigs as White Powder Mah in Thailand and General Phu Lau in Cambodia."

A quiet applause erupted from the group. Chu then raised his hand to halt the applause as he continued.

"We cannot move too quickly in our endeavors. Our movements must seem friendly to our competitors. So, in the beginning, proper protocols and favorable recognition given for these arrogant and unassuming potentates, honored. Then swept away swiftly before they respond."

Chu continued with his rhetoric and distaste at the old order of things.

"It is our duty and our mission. In consideration of the existing hierarchy present, they are sloppy and disorganized in their approach to their businesses, which will give way to our novel approach to efficiency and productivity."

"We must communicate this through our various

channels that we can offer substantial increases in productivity and distribution that will cause billions in revenue instead of the millions relating to their meager efforts."

"We will begin with the outer, less important elements of their hierarchy. Making it appear rising trends of disgruntlement exist within their ranks and has given rise to insurrection."

Chu went on.

"While we are sowing discontent, at the same time we will engender our hope and support for their difficulties with the centrists' leaders. We will offer them false hope as we create a false sense of security in our apparent unified bond. This will ensure a complacent attitude, making them unaware of their off-balance condition and vulnerability."

Again, the group applauded Chu's comments and plan for expansion for the rise and power of Hydra as the dominant force in the world.

Chu's sentinels requested a summit meeting, as official representatives of the newly formed Hydra Syndicate. The document delivered was like a traditional scroll handwritten by and signed by Chu, bound by a ribbon stamped with a gold medallion. Asian leaders dating back to the Ming dynasty still use this form of communique in a long-standing tradition.

The protocol is both a respectful acknowledgement of an adversary or competitor and an introductory appeasement to the known cultural and political differences within the various factions in the larger and more powerful crime organizations.

The Dragon Lady received the scroll and smiled. To her, it was a grand sign she may ultimately rise to the grand leader of all criminal clans in the future. This invitation clearly marked a new horizon for her criminal career. The choice of the meet would be hers, as stated in the document. She chose the center of her operations in Macau as her desired location. For security, both agreed it would be a food establishment in a populated area, but that the establishment would be devoid of any patrons on the eve of the meeting.

They set the stage for the potential alliance of the century between East and West. Such global alliances have not occurred since the great Khan, Tamojin organized all the Mongol tribes under his flag hundreds of years before.

The meeting would have occurred on the first day of Danwu, or the great Dragon Boat festival. This date suggestion, offered by the Dragon Lady, was a point of mutual respect to her Eastern competitor. Both felt this was auspicious. It would be a meeting of two dragons, the Dragon Lady and Doctor Chu, the Black Dragon.

It is a much-anticipated event by both parties entering the discussions with hidden agendas. Both parties will have their finest security guards present.

Meanwhile, Graywolf lay convalescing in a triage set up in London at a non- disclosed location by Nightshade. They treated Graywolf's wounds there from his confrontation with the Hydra ninjas.

He dreamed, standing around a militarized Humvee vehicle laughing at jokes with his Apache friends. The dream turns ugly as his friends stop laughing. Their faces turn gray. Their bodies fall apart in front of him, seeing the bloody parts strewn about on the ground. The Humvee is suddenly upside down and blown apart. His dream now turns to a full-blown nightmare.

He awakens still within his dream, lying on a gurney surrounded by surgeons and nurses at the army base hospital in Kandahar. He tried to ask questions, but no sound came from his lips. Then he tried to sit up, hoping to draw attention from those ignoring him. Graywolf could not raise himself up! He realized he had no forearms, just bandaged stumps ending at the elbows.

He wanted to scream but could not. A nurse nearby resembling his wife placed her hand on his shoulder. She spoke softly to comfort him from his shock and loss of limbs. His head fell back against the pillow, supporting him, tears streaming down his cheeks.

Then his body fell through the gurney down into a bottomless abyss. He tumbled over and over, with the bandages unraveling and flying away, exposing his ugly stumps. Again, he tried to scream but couldn't.

Black objects appeared to swim around him while he fell. It was raven wings separated and spinning around him. He desperately reached out to capture them, hoping the wings could break his fall into the never-ending abyss. After much struggling, he attached the wings to his stumps. Vigorously, he flapped to regain lost altitude. With one last thrust, he cawed in a loud screech, only to awake in a sweat. Graywolf sighed. He wiped the remaining tears from his face and looked down at his arms and legs, relieved to confirm he was intact. It was just a bad dream!

The first night of Danwu arrived. Dragon Lady feverishly prepared for the meet, attending to last-minute details regarding security and placing her arriving dignitaries at a table in a private dining area upstairs. She felt a second-floor location for the meet would also ease the tensions on both sides.

Dragon Lady was not naïve about her guests. Knowledge of Chu's treachery preceded him. If there were to be assassins about, the second-floor location would give her at least a few moments to prepare for such an intrusion.

The time for the meet was 6 o'clock. Dragon Lady told her soldier guards to take their places in both seen and unseen locations. Unlike her pre-emptive assault on her mentor's life, she eliminated her opposing clan members in one fell swoop. Here, she looks to encourage this alliance with aims to undermine Chu's power base and replace it with her own. Ironically, Doctor Chu's ambitions are not dissimilar.

Soon, three black Mercedes limos pulled up in front of the restaurant. Some people nearby stopped to look on as these gangsters rolled out of their black sedans. Each sported two flags from the fenders of each car waiving the Hydra symbol, seven dragon heads bound by a spider's web embroidered in gold against a black background. It appeared much like you would see in a presidential motorcade.

Chu was the last to exit as his supreme second repositioned his black silk overcoat more squarely over his shoulders. The other seconds formed around doctor Chu flanking him on both sides, forming a tight wedge as he entered the front entrance of the restaurant.

The restaurant owner was present to greet Chu and his henchmen bowing with respect, honor holding back feelings of fear for his life and the condition of his restaurant should a fight break out.

Doctor Chu stood waiting for the appearance of the Dragon Lady. She descended the staircase dressed in a solid white silk brocade sequenced dress, giving the appearance of a painted look to her slim body. The formal jacket hung below her hips, embroidered with golden threaded patterns of cherry blossoms and ferns. Her coal black hair pulled tightly back, revealing large, hooped rings dangling in a chain from each ear.

She approached Chu, extending her hand graciously. Chu committed to a pseudo kiss to the back of her hand while admonishing her Asian beauty and his favorite attribute, green eyes.

"Good evening, Madam Dragon. Your beauty is without measure and confirms all that I have heard about you. Of course, you possess the most treasured of attributes in my country. Your eyes are exquisite and beyond compare."

At that moment, Chu bowed his head, only to acknowledge her status. The Dragon Lady motioned to make way for Chu and his party to ascend the stairs to the room of their meeting.

All seconds stood waiting around the table for Chu and the Dragon Lady to arrive. Sitting down before their leaders have taken their seat would be a great embarrassment. It would surely mean for them, perhaps, losing a finger or worse, their head later.

The Dragon Lady waited for Chu to sit before she took her seat. Chu's supreme second removed his outer coat to reveal his long coat, also heavily embroidered with golden dragons, rising next to the lapels of his coat. The jacket collar rose straight forward into a classic Neru design. Smaller dragons wrapped around his collar, giving the appearance of embracing his neck.

He wore a classic bright red silk hat like Mandarin rulers, fitted with a black tassel draped over one side. He removed his hat and placed on the table near him and sat down with grace and obvious confidence.

He sported a classic goat tee beard. The mustache was narrow. The chin beard was also narrow and cut very thin, showing a mixture of gray and black color.

The Dragon Lady began by illustrating her knowledge of Chu's businesses and various operations in the East. She followed by outlining some of her holdings and operations.

So, the negotiations began by discussing how their operations could work along-side, each with an overriding agreement to join forces to both their advantages.

No food got served during the meeting, but they shared a final cordial drink to seal their agreements.

Chu then left, confident of the façade he had presented to the Dragon Lady. After the Chu's party left, the Dragon Lady sat with her closest seconds to discuss their strategy in dealing Chu in the future. Chu had spies everywhere. She needed to be cautious of her movements.

The caravan of limos sped quickly away. Chu took a few chances with security. He told the drivers to take several narrow back streets leading onto the Jing Gang'ao Expressway to avoid an ambush. Chu turned to his supreme second, Lin Pao.

"Lin, I want to hack Dragon Lady's loan business accounts and locate her prostitution houses. Stir up resentment by beating up some of her more beautiful girls. Destroy their faces, so they will be useless. Have your captains sow labor discontent among her lower workers to create labor shutdowns and other conflicts. She will become very distracted as we pit one clan against another."

Pao, you must make these systematic attacks appear random. We do not want to reveal our intentions too early. You will find out what her courier routes are, intercept her couriers and pose as their replacements to short the collection of payments. Finally, we must find her personal bank. That will be your ultimate target. The ensuing chaos will be our right hand to undermine the other clan's desire to support her as well.

"It won't take long. Then, I will watch her

organization fall out of her control as we move in quietly and consume the entire Macau Syndicate. Now will be the time to assassinate our old friend, White Powder Mah. The Dragon Lady will then need to renegotiate her treaties with the remaining opium producers. She has been lazy! She will not know the other producers very well. Then we can secretly replace the other producers with our own producers and she will never know."

"All this will slow down her drug trade long enough to weaken her finances. Chu grinned. She will fill our coffers with her profits."

Pao smiled and nodded in approval.

Meanwhile, the Dragon Lady left the restaurant with her seconds only minutes after Chu's exit. She told the driver to make a stop at one of her drop locations to discuss changes in routes taken by her couriers. She expected Chu's attempt to infiltrate her ranks and instructed the couriers to use new codes from now on to determine and establish better security.

Meanwhile, Graywolf recovered sufficiently to attend a gathering of Nightshade's finest shadow warriors.

Several miles outside of London was a large abbey on several hundred acres of hunting grounds. The Duke of Windsor previously owned the estate and property and looked to sell. Nightshade purchased the abbey and grounds at this location to provide an excellent cover for their clandestine European-Asian Operations Headquarters.

The abbey and grounds sported a legitimate front as a fox and hound hunting club. The main drawing room of the abbey became the conference room. Walls surrounding the drawing room displayed several paintings of fox hunts during the history of the abbey, other portraits of the club's membership prominently displayed. An enormous fireplace adorned the center of the west wall. The air in the room smelled of stale cigar smoke mixed with the smell of the soot in the fireplace.

In the middle of the meeting room was a very long, dark-wooded gothic table. On the tabletop, a leather sheath dressed in the center, with leather tufted seats spread evenly all around. The conference room table could accommodate over forty members present.

The moderate hum of voices subsided into silence. The meeting was about to begin. One of the less specific agendas related to exploring new strategies to deal with the rapidly changing criminal landscape. Some agents wanted to be more specific. There were certain individuals whose power had sped up to new heights and influence. That influence was spreading too quickly, even into higher political and economic circles.

Bickering broke out between several agents over the importance of their various concerns. The Lieutenant-Colonel in charge attending the meeting, named Harper, came from Nightshade Corporate to intervene, explaining.

"We are here to find out the levels of importance regarding all the issues brought forth. The purpose of this meeting, he went on, is to determine how they are we to distribute assets. How much to distribute? When and where should they distribute?"

The disgruntled agents sat back in their

respective chairs and joined the unanimous feeling of perspective and focus presented by the Lieutenant-Colonel.

The acquiescence toward those important persons became the most significant, yet not unrelated to the overview that some also wanted to discuss.

Agent Florez stood and declared.

"My team has been tailing a woman said to have taken over control of the Macau Syndicate. She goes by the name of Dragon Lady."

Some of the group connected more heavily to the European theater, chuckled at her name. Then agent Midh Ghan of the Hong Kong contingent spoke in defense.

"Do not laugh, my friends. This woman handles the death of many of our agents. She is quite cunning and very dangerous. Unfortunately, two of those casualties were from my team!" Silence fell upon the room, only to give way to another agent from Taiwan.

Jong Li then stood to add.

"There is another growing menace that poses an even greater threat. Based on our investigations, this new group may try to merge with the Triads. We tried to penetrate this growing cancer out of Beijing, but we got stonewalled at every turn and suffered many losses so far. We still know little about this group, but the leader's name is Doctor Fu Wung Chu."

Jong motioned for a projection of slides of Chu with Chiang Kai Shek.

"What little we know is; he served with Chen's General, Chiang Kai Shek during the war. Later, became a billionaire industrialist brokering weapons between middle-eastern countries and warring factions in Africa."

"There are rumors he possesses a fortress protected by a private army on an island somewhere in the South China sea. If it exists, it does not show up on any maps or charts to date."

"This Chu character arrived in Taiwan a few months ago to attend a meeting with other industrialists. On the surface, it looks legit. They all checkout. They apparently want to discuss Taiwan's future in a global economy with the West. We noticed a rise in local skirmishes between Triad factions soon after he arrived here. We cannot confirm this, but we think this Chu guy is trying to muscle in on the Triad syndicate."

Then the Lieutenant-Colonel commended Jong for their great detective work.

The Lieutenant commented.

"It would seem we have two contenders for our attention. Let us bring to bear upon these two people our full attention and resources. Perhaps there is some connection that leads to further discovery, that either an alliance or a war may be on afoot."

Meanwhile, the Dragon Lady, feeling confident she has shored up her defenses against Doctor Chu's aggressions, she learns to disturb news of labor disputes among the chefs of her restaurants. Even more upsetting was to learn that some girls in some houses have suffered brutal attacks recently from clientele.

She grimaced with her teeth clenched tightly, saying.

"No one messes with my girls. I will sort this out!"

Chu's plan was brilliant. The Dragon Lady could not see beyond the false premise that all the chaos was only random. He joked at one point, saying.

"Some say it is the moon making everyone crazy. But this has been going on for months now and there are only a few days of full moonlight. So, I believe the idea that it's the moon causing this is beyond imagination!"

As Dragon Lady sat at the viewing console, fourteen monitors scanned each of her lab/drop off locations for unusual activity or trouble. The system could scan both visibly and with infrared. Feeling bored, she switched to the internal internet to review assets and receipts records for the past six months. On a hunch, she identified Chu's
license plate number, track its whereabouts, all at the time of these raids.

To her amazement, she saw a pattern of coincidence with Chu's presence within half a mile of each area of attack. Then she thought.
"I knew that motherf***er was up to something. I could feel it." She reached down along-side her right thigh and extracted her nine-millimeter

strapped to her leg.

She rubbed her face against the barrel of the pistol and said.

"And… I'm going to make you feel this barrel up your ass, Doctor Chu, or whatever your name is! That's my final parting of this arrangement."

She closed the door of the console room, grabbed her briefcase and top coat to head toward the front of the building. Her car was already waiting for her arrival.

Her voice print and retinal scanner could only access the entrance. The quarters lay deep inside a compound protected by another layer of staff armed with automatic weapons.

Inside the courtyards grew small forest evergreens surrounded by other lush vegetation. The density of foliage could compare to a normal jungle. Her habitat was near to the office of the supreme second, where she reviewed comings and goings of her lab/drop off locations and her server containing her productivity records, showing profits and losses.

She casually dropped her coat on top of her

briefcase, which sat precariously on the edge of her coffee table. Being slightly anal, she would respond accordingly. This minor infraction of neatness and balance would have to wait. She needed to think about what she may have discovered regarding Chu. The Dragon Lady thought. "I could always think more clearly with at least one or two belts of good bourbon."

Her head turned to gaze upon the decanter of bourbon sitting along the back wall of the bar. She sauntered up to the bar and filled a glass with a little ice. She poured until the glass was full. After shooting down two gulps of whiskey, she gritted her teeth, commenting.

"Damn, that's good bourbon!"

She dropped into her settee next to her bed with a drink well in hand. The glass had become chilled from the ice. An idea that coolness might help a headache. She rubbed her brow with the cold glass. Soon she realized it was only making her head and possibly her hair wet. That would not do! Besides, it was irritating.

As Dragon Lady considered her options, that her

actions had to be slow and cautious. She needed reconnaissance of Chu's activities. Perhaps, if she tailed him, she might gather the evidence of his treachery. She could not move on Chu until she had proof, otherwise the other clans would rebuke her for not accepting proper protocol. They might accuse her of breaking the truce of territorial claims settled years ago amongst all the Triad clans. That's the trouble she doesn't need right now.

Meanwhile, Chu, satisfied that his subversive actions have substantially weakened Dragon Lady's strength. Now was the time Chu attacked all of her strongholds. Also, his intel revealed the location of her personal bank and so, while his men were busy wiping out many of her defenders, he planned to break open her safe.

Having tracked Chu's destination, Dragon Lady issued commands to her supreme second and to all of his captains to fight to the death to defend their syndicate holdings. Then she told her supreme second, Hai Sung, to remain with her along with one of his captains, Li Wan.

Hai said.

"Madam boss, it's no longer safe for you. There is danger of a breach. So we need to get you to safety."

Dragon Lady responded.

"No Hai, you and Li must come with me. I want to catch Chu red handed. Then I will be justified in his murder. He is headed for my vault in the Sang Han district. I want to get there before he arrives to make for a surprise confrontation."

"Bring my car around. We must hurry!" She said urgently.

Hai drove, racing through the back streets, knowing a shorter way to her vault location. It was an old warehouse used for making garments. The main floor held several sowing stations and a large loom for weaving raw materials. The second floor suspended the office high above the main floor, providing the high ground. She hoped that an early arrival would give her the advantage.

They pulled up to the rear entrance and rushed into the building, making their way to the stairs leading to the office above. Li put the lights on and Dragon Lady stopped him.

"No Li, we must not give Chu a sign we are on to his plan."

Li bowed his head and replied.

"Sorry, Madam Boss."

Hai went first, followed by the Dragon Lady, now holding her pistol by her side.
Li followed to protect their rear position. The staircase leading to the office was dark. The office door was closed, giving the appearance they were the first to arrive.

Hai opened the door slowly, and Dragon Lady moved quickly beyond Hai into the room. The desk lamp switched on, unexpectedly revealing Doctor Chu and several of his men. Dragon Lady got startled and raised her pistol and fired at Chu, only wounding him in the shoulder.

Chu's men openly fired with their automatic weapons, spraying the room with a hail of bullets, taking Hai and Li to the floor. Dragon Lady also fell to her knees, bleeding badly from her abdomen. As she weaved her eyes closed for a moment.
She could hear Doctor Chu comment.

"Clearly, Madam Dragon, you cannot stop the

inevitable truth. My skills are far greater than yours, and that makes me a better choice to command your clans."

The Dragon Lady smiled and replied.

"I'm not finished yet!"

Her body relinquished the kneeling position and collapsed to the floor. She had pulled from her coat, her cell phone. She smiled slightly as she entered send to the code for explosives set as a last resort. Then, in her last breath, she uttered.

"Goodbye Doctor Chu. Our bargain, finished."

Then she pushed the send button, and the office separated from the second floor in a great blast. All of Chu's men sailed into the air. Their body parts flying to the floor, while Chu, still standing behind the vault door, got pushed out of a nearby window and landed upon Dragon lady's car. He rolled onto the ground unconscious, but still alive.

Chu's men came running and swooped up his body. He spoke in a weakened voice.

"Wait! We must recover Dragon Lady's head for proof of her demise before we leave here. Then we can arrange a meet with the other Triad clans to form the new alliance of Triads with Hydra."

Chu passed out again in the car as they headed swiftly for his doctor.

Nightshade coupled their surveillance onto the Chinese communication satellite known as Queqiao (Magpie Bridge) using an unused side channel. Their liaison at Interpol provided possible coordinates for the unknown island fortress known as Nemesis.

There were three coordinates in the South China sea for the target. After several hours of analysis, Nightshade decided that only one fit the known attributes for Nemesis. The Lieutenant then ordered a Phase 1 assault. This type of assault would not include an air and land coordinated effort. Surprise was essential to the mission's success. So, the only way in was by sea.

An approach by several hundred underwater scuba divers would approach by the eastern side of the island. The satellite reconnaissance showed the eastern side of the island and considered the most plausible for their plan of attack. Guards were few on that side because of the difficulty of scaling the 200-foot cliff leading to the fortress. They hollowed the cliff beneath the rim. This meant that a free climb aim, though extremely difficult, was the only choice available.

The scuba divers needed to be excellent swimmers as well. They would begin their journey ten miles from shore, off-loaded from a tramp steamer moored at sea. The divers needed to be class four climbers as well, to ascend the ceiling of the cliff from underneath. The eastern side of the island was also the windward side, where the sea would prove to be an additional challenge. Surf was violent, constantly crashing against large protruding rocks that spread beneath the cliff.

The assault also included one more hindrance. It needed to be at night. They equipped all the divers with night-vision equipment they carried in back packs under their scuba gear. Five of the divers were leading point on the assault and were first to arrive to assess the risk and determine the best position to prepare for the ascent to the upper surface.

The Lieutenant was on the com link to the first five divers waiting for their report back to the command center aboard the steamer and command center also kept track of possible Chinese interference if the mission became compromised.

The lieutenant knew the mission parameters were less than ideal and expected a sixty-five percent chance of success. He was even less optimistic about casualties,expecting fifty percent losses during the surface engagement.

Each soldier-diver could only hand carry most of the weaponry. The automatic weapons they carried had grenade launchers mounted below the barrel of the gun as an over-under configuration. They filled their vests with multiple clips loaded with bullets specially crafted for armor piercing ability, containing an unusually high grain of powder offering long range capability as a sniper would use. This ammo would support the penetration of heavily armored vehicles and powerful defenses in the fortress.

Though an air assault by predator drones would have been swift and effective, the political and military implications of violating Chinese airspace on approach would certainly end up in an international incident and be difficult to contain. The collateral impact of the Chinese government was unacceptable.

While the scuba divers prepared to descend into the water, two Chinese fighters scrambled from the newly constructed airstrip on the Subi Reef in the Spratly Islands, sent to investigate the tramp steamer. They were fourth generation Changdu J-20 jets equipped with sophisticated infrared scanners. The steamer, suspiciously moored within Chinese occupied waters. The tramp steamer was flying a United Arab Emirates flag with registration permits to carry oil drilling equipment representing Saudi interests. Radio contact from Chinese reconnaissance requested justification of the ship's business while sitting in their waters.

As previously considered in Nightshade's strategy, if vehement protests were to arise, the ship's captain could achieve additional time. They instructed him to explain that the ship's engines were giving them trouble and needed repairs. The explanation resulted in a negotiation. They would set an expected demand and a limit for those repairs. The demand limited the delay to forty-eight hours. Then steps took by the Chinese government to intercede, towing the freighter with an escort to the nearest port for boarding and inspection by the Chinese military.

Nightshade expected this possibility. The Lieutenant felt that forty-eight hours would be an acceptable parameter for the mission. As night fell upon the ship, they slipped twenty rubber rafts into the sea along with one hundred divers.

Meanwhile, Doctor Chu expected the possibility that his island would eventually be revealed, leading to an eventual assault on his island fortress. He rigged the fortress with plastic explosives in critical areas surrounding the fortress walls and in secure areas inside. He also prepared his captains with counter-insurgency plans if an assault could occur.

He mounted several fifty-caliber machine gun turrets on top of the five towers strategically positioned on the fortress walls. The fortress, built by Taoist oriented engineers eight-hundred years before, based it upon Five Element Theory. Chu felt confident that this defense concept worked well for the early Chinese emperors seeking a private refuge in case of a revolt. It would work for Chu now as well.

When the divers were within reach of the island perimeter, they discovered several mines distributed along the coastal waters. More important was a heavy steel net that barricaded the sea entrance. The divers faced a dilemma. They could not go over the net above the surface without being discovered.

Chu was aware of the mines and net planted by the Chinese many years before, providing his island with additional defenses. The ten-mile mooring location kept the freighter clear of the mines, but the net was a serious problem.

During the warfare tactics used during the Chinese-Japanese conflict, the island airstrip needed to be secured. They installed the net to prevent a sneak attack on the island by Japanese submarines. This net prevented their using the coastal waters as an adequate cover for their approach to the cliff. They had no choice but to cut through the net. This additional problem severely curtailed the diver's approach efforts. Cutting the net would use up precious time for many hours.

The divers did not adequately prepare for this

obstruction. It forced them to use their supplies of specially impregnated phosphorus cord to cut an opening into the net. The phosphorus cord was effective, but would eliminate the planned use of the cord to enter more secured areas inside the fortress. The divers still needed time to prepare for their climb to the cliff summit.

Twenty-five hours passed. Only part of the net now breached. The lead team surfaced long enough to report of their difficulty with the obstacle and limited success. After successfully breaching the net, only eight hours remained for the cliff ascent and penetration into the fortress.

When the lead team emerged, the violent surf smashed two of the divers onto the rocks, killing them instantly. The other three had to ignore their loss and proceeded on to the ground beneath the cliff. They quickly removed their scuba gear and suits and prepared the ascent ropes, anchoring them to the nearby rocks. Many other divers emerged then joining their comrades in the ascent preparations. As the first team began their climb, others held the ropes tight on the ground. Pitons were driven into the rocks along the cliff wall, coordinated by the pounding of the surf, keeping the sound of their hammering as quiet as possible. After two hours, most of the divers were halfway up toward the summit.

Two of the pitons came loose, causing five divers to plummet to their deaths. The pounding surf masked their impact on the surface. They dared not scream in their descent for fear of revealing their presence. The members of the first team reached the summit, crouching below the rocks on the rim until they could assess the presence and location of the perimeter guards.

As the guards passed, they attacked them using only their knives to cut their throats. Then they hoisted their comrades until all reached the summit.

The walls of the fortress were thirty feet high and needed to be scaled as well. Two lead members fired air-powered grappling hooks into the air, fastening to the parapets along the upper wall. One diver secured the grappling hook rope while the others began their ascent of the fortress wall.

There was a small pathway behind the parapet which provided cover to the climbers. The remaining divers crouched low inside the pathway until all were on top of the fortress wall. Then ropes tossed to the grounds inside, with the divers scaling downward five at a time.

Soon after the last divers, they spread out, hurrying to their targets. They eliminated the surprise after they fired the first shots. The grenades exploded. Machine gun turrets open fired with a hail of bullets spraying the lower area.
Several divers fell to the ground. They blew two turrets up, and the assault was now well underway.
Then planted explosives ignited, killing more divers.

The remaining divers made it to the main building, killing many of Chu's men along the way. They escorted Chu to the escape route he had designed into the fortress.

The fortress contained several cisterns below the compound. Chu prepared one cistern with a tunnel and canal leading to the sea. There, waiting, was a small submarine capable of carrying three men. Chu and two of his lieutenants made their way into the secret cistern following the canal to the docked submarine. They boarded the submarine, quickly closing the hatch behind them. The sub escaped without notice, leaving behind them the ongoing chaos above.

Chu and his two lieutenants successfully made their way to Singapore, where a private docking station awaited their arrival. His plan to re-enter Hong Kong clandestinely was via his personal jet at a private airstrip in Singapore.

Meanwhile, Nightshade's assault successfully destroyed Chu's compound on Nemesis Island. Unfortunately, Chu and his key lieutenants escaped the attack. Nightshade had one disadvantage. They could not identify Chu. The goal was to eliminate Chu and many of his captains, thus crippling Hydra's operations. The possibility that Chu might have eluded their assault troubled the Lieutenant. He also suspected a leak about the assault plan within Nightshade. This troubled him more.

They arranged an emergency meeting in London to discuss the blowback from Chu and his organization. Essentially, Hydra was still very much intact and operations throughout the region were essentially undisturbed by the attack on the island compound. Now their operations would have tightened security. Word reached Nightshade from friendly informants. They promised to double down on plans to retaliate.

Nightshade abandoned their open warfare approach. Once again, they planned to rely on their inner group of Shadow Warriors to infiltrate Chu's defenses, to pursue the goal of assassinating Chu and his lieutenants.

Graywolf and other warriors were part of the meeting. They invited the Shadow Warriors to give their appraisal of how to accomplish an insurgency into Chu's organization. Many expressed concern that they may be out-numbered and overwhelmed. Graywolf added.

"Lieutenant, he began, we still have surveillance on many of his operations and we have ongoing feedback on the street. If Chu makes any moves, this may soon reveal his safe-houses and their probable locations. The caveat, of course, it won't be easy. He will be a moving target now."

The lieutenant nodded in agreement.

"Do not worry. We'll get him." He said with conviction to Graywolf.

Meanwhile, Chu called for a meeting with the Captains of the Triads. For safety and secrecy, the meeting occurred in an abandoned strip mine deep in the countryside. The agenda was to rally the troops, reassure the captains of his leadership, reminding them about his swift demise of the Dragon Lady. News of his stronghold on Nemesis shocked and confused many in the out-lying districts. Rumors had spread that Chu died in the assault.

Chu began.

"Well gentlemen, Chu said with a grin, news of my demise got exaggerated!" Everyone burst into laughter at his sarcastic tone.

"We need to focus on our business. Let us consider this attack as merely a brief interruption. Business will continue as usual. However, no one knows what I look like, especially those who run the Nightshade operation. They have become an irritant. So deceit will be a much-needed ally now. We will assist with the illusion that someone indeed murdered me at my compound in Nemesis. Our re-organization will give the appearance that Hydra has lost its heads and now scurries about to operate without me. This will engender false confidence and their guard will be relaxed."

"Instead of consolidating, we will take all of our operations and model them after our friends within the Hezbollah guard of Iraq and Iran. We will disperse into the night, operating as well-organized cells."

"I have reprogrammed these cell phones with a new encryption algorithm." As he spoke, he gestured to those present to pick them up.

He continued speaking while they paraded by the table. His lieutenants and captains listened intently as Chu continued.

"These phones work with a unique frequency encoding process unknown by any of the anti-crime units. This will allow our cells to function in the meantime with certain freedom."

Chu continued.

"We will target first those areas of law enforcement in the region with the most strategic installations. Those that have cyber-espionage capabilities with satellite uplinks. This will minimize their involvement in our activities."

Meanwhile, after his loyal subjects left, Chu retreated to his secret chamber hidden below ground behind the mine shaft. A side path near the mine's main entrance accessed the cloaked chamber. A fake support with a built-in lever replaced one support for the mine. Access to the lever was through an electrical junction box mounted on the fake support post.

After careful deliberation, Chu decided it was time to implement the use of forces from the Dark Forge. Learning about the Dark Forge was one of the key gifts from his master, the Dark Lord Asmodius. Calling upon the realm of the Dark Forge was risky even for him. He did not consider this move lightly. It could have far-reaching consequences for him personally.

As much as he dismissed the importance of the impact of his stronghold being breached, it disturbed him. Chu always kept his own counsel, he never revealed his inner feelings, even to his closest allies. Chu was very concerned that his plan of dominion in the criminal world might go badly with a rush to judgement to orchestrate strong retaliatory moves. It could deplete his forces that were at his disposal. He realized he needed something more. Something he felt would be an effective countermeasure against anything that Nightshade might dream of.

These formidable energies, he controlled, he can now summon. Chu was a great sorcerer and commanded the strength of certain very dangerous demons. These demons were powerful and ranked very high within the realm of the great darkness. These demons are those same demons in which King Solomon once commanded to assist in his battles against his enemies. They will serve those who have the knowledge and skill to speak the secret words of power. Chu had that knowledge. He also possessed the skill to speak those secret angelic words that few on the planet could wield.

He summoned Asmodeus, King of the Dark Forge. Soon, three of his minions appeared. Balor, demon of the wind, Berith, demon of the fire and Tumbir, demon of the water.

Chu stood in his power circle and demanded.

"I command you thou Marquis of the Dark Forge, Amadeus appears now before me!"

The three minions cried out together.

"Oh, lord of the earth, our master is not available, so he sent us to greet you and answer your call."

Chu raised his arms and shouted the power words three times. The minions cried out again.

"Oh, Lord of the earth, please let us attend to thy needs, lest our master will castigate us."

Again, Chu raised his arms and shouted.

"Amadeus, thou art my servant! I command you and only you to do my bidding! Appear Marquis of the Dark Forge."

Then he struck his scepter to the ground and spoke the ultimate words of power. Soon the ground shook with a violent rumble and the King of the Dark Forge appeared only partially, showing eyes of fire.

Asmodeus whirled fiercely about Chu's circle with his fiery eyes glaring at Chu. Then the king of the demons cried out.

"Why do you summon me in this way? You have used the greater words which you know causes us great pain!"

Chu knew that to use those words would forever alter their relationship. Chu had enjoyed a mutual respect from the great demon. It was more like two great chess masters testing their wits with each other, always ending with a draw.

It was a bold move requiring courage beyond human frailty and was tantamount to scolding the king of the demons. Yet, he stood firm knowing if he were to show the slightest weakness, Asmodeus would strip Chu's body of his skin, dismember him and devour him on the spot, circle or no.

Asmodeus' tone returned with a distinct unfriendly and sinister quality Chu had not experienced from the demon king before.

"You have taken a grave step, wizard. We have always admired your cunning, your brutality, and your ruthlessness. We have always honored your humble requests before, without recompense. Did you not escape the torrent brought upon your island repose? We gave you the gift of invisibility along with greater success in all your endeavors. This time is different! Your demand takes on a different dimension and will have consequences ultimately!"

"You would be wise to back down from this demand. Yet, if you persist, then we will hear your petition wizard."

Chu began.

"Great and powerful Asmodeus, I come with a demand as the conditions that surround me call for more serious needs that only you can provide. These needs are urgent. Hence, why I have commanded you with a demand, to show you the severity of my situation. The forces of light have surrounded and threatened my business concerns and even encroached upon the sanctity of an otherwise fruitful existence on the earth."

Asmodeus spoke again with a thunderous voice.

"I meet your demand with an equal demand. You hold in your possession three objects of great power, which bind us to your will. If we agree to your demand, then you must give up those objects and release the binding tie between us forever more. If you force this bargain, then we are bound to force you into a bargain of equal nature. You understand this?

"You know of what objects we speak? The Jade Dragon, the ring of Solomon the king and finally, the golden trine of serpents that bind the opal jewel that captures our secret name. You cannot speak the greater words of power without also yielding to this forfeiture. To refuse is not in the order of things!"

Chu gritted his teeth and responded.

"Great Asmodeus, you know that would relieve me of the protection from all forces bent on my destruction, including from you and the Dark Forge. What assurances do I have from you that you would not retaliate against me soon after I relinquish those possessions?"

The king of demons leaned in on the circle where Chu stood and said in a low and ominous tone.

"NONE!"

The demon went on.

"Is it not what we have always told you? Greater rewards must also come with greater risks?"

Chu bowed his head but did not take his eyes away from the demon. He knew even in battles between mere human martial combatants; They always transfix the eyes upon one's opponent at all times, lest the opponent outwit the other as they lower their guard.

Chu was foolish enough to actually think he could outwit the demon in his bargain. Then, with confidence built upon his arrogance, Chu answered the demon.

"All right, I agree to your terms."

The demon finally showed his horrible face with a grimacing smile, showing many razor-sharp fangs, and said solemnly.

"So be it, so let it be said and so let it be done. Now what are your demands, wizard?"

Chu reasoned with his thoughts.

"First, I want to be invincible and impervious to any harm that may come my way. Second, I want control of your three minions, Balor, Berith and Tumbir. I want to control wind, fire and water whenever I will it."

Asmodeus then paused and replied.

"All right wizard, I will grant your needs on one condition. You will have these at your beck and call, but only for six of your years. These minions are precious to us, and we will not let go of them forever. Do you agree to our terms?"

Chu nodded to affirm his agreement. In that moment, the light from the surrounding candles extinguished abruptly and the great demon was gone. Chu let out a sigh of relief. Then, in that moment, his body tingled, and he felt a surge of energy rushing through his spine.

Chu needed to confirm the demon had kept his word. So, he pulled his dagger from its sheath and held out his hand, and brought the blade to bear in his palm. He gripped the blade as he pulled it sharply through his grip. Then he opened his hand and watched closely as his blood poured freely from the open wound.

For a moment, he felt Asmodeus had cheated on him. Then the bleeding stopped, and the gaping wound in his palm sealed before his eyes. There was no pain and no sign that he had cut into his flesh.

Now he was ready.

Counter-terrorist operations by Nightshade to pursue Doctor Chu and his nefarious activities involved multiple crime investigations from several national and international organizations like Interpol, Massad, the National Police Agency of Japan and included nationally are the anti-terrorist units of the National Security Agency, the FBI and the CIA.

Despite combined efforts to use satellites and drone surveillance brought nothing to the table. Chu became a ghost to all of them. When the intel would reveal likely locations for Chu's whereabouts, raids on those locations always turned up empty. Only minor minions of his organization got caught and captured. Despite severe interrogation techniques on those soldiers, revealed little or nothing significant to help their efforts to capture or kill the main kingpins of the Hydra organization.

After six years of intense effort by Nightshade, the extreme pursuit of Chu and his lieutenants and Captains proved futile. Then all the files got placed into the 'cold' category, awaiting possible new leads on the case. Nightshade continued with their investigations, but placed more emphasis on other criminal activities.

Graywolf had a time of coming. He went to have a beer with a couple of his shadow warrior buddies at one of the local beer gardens in Hong Kong. They were relaxed and soon one beer turned into a few.

Their booth was next to another booth where several Chinese were busy with some of the bar girls encouraging them to buy more drinks. The sound from an automated kiosk located nearby the beer garden prompted some locals to join in singing to American lyrics from eighties pop culture music filling the room with bad karaoke providing painful and often off-key renditions.

Graywolf recognized the attempt to reproduce one of his favorite songs before the war. He felt old memories returning. Thoughts wondering what might have been about the life he had on the Res. He felt sadness and remorse for losing his fiancé and their plans to have a child after he returned from Iraq.

He became quiet, wincing at the poorly showed

vocals as tears filled his eyes. His friends joked when he mourned the badly sung music. He laughed a little at their jokes while they tried to cheer him up. Then he decided he wanted something stronger than beer. As he headed for the bar, his friends joked again about 'Injuns' staying away from the firewater.

He sat next to a Chinese National already well engrossed in Hong Kong's version of a Mai-Tai cocktail. Specialty drinks were typically heavy on the alcohol, and this man was obviously dipping into his fourth drink. He slumped over the bar, appearing to be only partly cogent. He wasn't saying much and seemed disgruntled.

Graywolf decided he would buy another round for the troubled stranger. When the drink arrived, the stranger looked up through bloodshot eyes and smiled slightly toward Graywolf while tipping the glass to his lips. Then he mumbled something, but Graywolf could not make out what he was saying. So, Graywolf engaged further and asked.

"What's that you said? With all the noise, I could not hear you, friend."

Then the stranger turned and repeated.

"I'm a total failure! Now I can no longer support my mistress. As he continued with slurred speech. I love her more than my wife. She is a bitch and now I'm stuck with her!"

Graywolf became curious and inquired why. The stranger went into unconsciousness and slumped forward, exposing an odd tattoo. It was a triangle wrapped in an embrace by two serpents and in the middle was an eye with fire burning above it.

At first, he thought a little about it. Then realized he was sitting next to a captain of one of Hydra's clan. "But how could this be? He thought. This guy looks like a bagman on the entry level, yet his tattoo shows he is a clan leader!" who got presently trashed in a beer garden.

Then Graywolf shook him and tell the stranger he has to go home.
The stranger got up with a Neanderthal grunt, then declared he was about to be sick! Graywolf said.

"It's all right ole man. I'll make sure you get home. Speaking of which, where do you live anyway?"

Then the stranger came alert just long enough to

explain that he lives only a block away from the beer garden. Graywolf then suspended his body under his arm enough, so that they could more or less walk to his flat.

The stranger's flat actually was not his home. This space is where he and his mistress could be together undisturbed. The entrance was three steps up from the level of the street. His flat was located one block away. His street was parallel to the street from where they stood. It descended and sloped down at an angle. The two stumbled along until they reached his flat entrance.

His flat was in the middle of an industrial compound with several large warehouses. The entrance of his flat was just down the street from of one of those warehouses.

Just as Graywolf began to handoff the stranger to the door of his flat, two black limos pulled up in front of the warehouse next door. Four soldiers stepped out, making way for the very important person, about to step out of the limo onto the street. He gaped with widened eyes to see before him, the infamous Doctor Fu Wan Chu standing not thirty meters from him. Quickly, Chu and his Captains and lieutenants all entered the warehouse.

Graywolf entered in a panic. There was no time or availability to call in an airstrike on the warehouse. He was alone. He ran through the odds of a successful single man assault against ten well-armed men, and then there is that unknown factor his gut is now screaming about.

"What about Chu? Who is he? Does he possess supernatural abilities?"

Graywolf reasoned, perhaps it is the wrong move to take Chu out without proper authorization. Then again, Nightshade would tear out their nails if they knew where he was at and what he faced in this critical moment.

The most he could hope for, in this dilemma, he would accomplish what all the others could not. He realized his courage and fortitude were on the rise as his feeling that a worthy sacrifice may be in order here, meaning himself. He felt he needed to take the shot, to engage, swearing to do what is required of him for the sake of the everlasting light.

He turned to the drunk captain, shoving him

against his door, saying.

"Have a better night."

He turned to face the street occupied by the two sedans. The drivers stayed outside in readiness to leave quickly and leaned against their respective vehicles to have a cigarette. As he approached, they stopped talking. Graywolf decided on shapeshifting, but he needed cover. He spotted a small vestibule next to the flat where he dropped off the drunk captain.

He ducked into the vestibule long enough to change his human form and then flew out, circling overhead, looking for an entrance to the warehouse. He spotted a small window that was tilted open slightly, allowing him a stealthy entrance. Then he circled above and then landed on one of the wood rafters.

Graywolf assessed the situation while Chu was talking with one of his producers. He counted six soldiers present along with the two captains and lieutenant standing nearby.

Graywolf waited to see if he could separate the soldiers from the rest and Chu. After several minutes, Graywolf realized the meeting was about to end and he had little time to strike.

He darted downward in a full dive, with talons out. He attacked two of the soldiers, blinding them in one strike. As gunfire spread across the ceiling, Graywolf flew in a zig-zag pattern, avoiding their retaliation. Then headed straight for another gunman pecking at his hand holding his weapon. Then the gunman dropped his weapon, grabbing his bleeding hand. As he stooped to recover his gun, Graywolf flapped his wings in the gunman's face and then struck him in the left eye, plucking it from its socket. Quickly swooping in a tight curve, he caught another gunman and landed on his head, pecking furiously at his scalp. As he fought to remove the enormous bird from his head, Graywolf leaned over his brow and struck him in both eyes, blinded him.

Then, in an instant, he transformed back into his human form. Now, he engaged the other two soldiers physically in a rapid succession of punches and kicks, rendering them unconscious.

Meanwhile, Chu had stepped back cautiously, leaving his lieutenant and two captains as his front guards, while he examined Graywolf in action. Graywolf made several flips in the air and ricocheted off some crates nearby to assault the two captains from their flank.

When he landed, his foot swept one captain, kicking him in the head and knocked him out. The other captain made several high kicks in retaliation. The first kick missed, but the captain reversed his position quickly and connected a powerful blow, dropping Graywolf to the floor. Graywolf recovered quickly, however, and countered with two powerful punches to his chest and gut. He ended this fight with a full roundhouse kick to his face, taking him out of the equation.

Now Graywolf stood facing Chu, with Chu's lieutenant holding a pistol aimed at Graywolf. The lieutenant fired off two rounds, but they trained Graywolf to listen for the intermediary phalanx bones of the gunman's forefinger, changing pressure on the trigger of his weapon. Anticipating in advance, the bullets leaving the barrel of his gun. He easily avoided the harm and moved out of the way.

Chu commanded his lieutenant to stand down. He would deal with Graywolf in his own way. He first praised Graywolf with his supernatural prowess.

"Well, it seems we face with a clever and formidable foe here. However, as good as you might be, young warrior, your talents are no match for my skills in battle."

Graywolf smiled nervously as he gritted his teeth for the battle of his life. He took a stance of offensive posture to prepare for Chu's attack. Chu also assumed an attack posture, but then he outstretched his palms in claw like fashion, offering the appearance of a Tiger-Crane fighting form. But then Chu's palms became bright red and a billowing column of fire rushed out to Graywolf, burning his clothing. Chu began spraying the area with fire as though he had possession of a flamethrower.

Graywolf avoided Chu's attacks with fire. Then he saw Chu waving his arms in large circles, muttering unknown sounds while still holding his hands as claws. He prepared himself for more fire when suddenly, a strong wind consumed Graywolf, throwing his body through the air thirty feet into a stack of wooden crates.

Now Graywolf realized he was dueling with a master sorcerer. He raised himself up from the floor, only to find himself awash with a wall of water from Chu. He lay unconscious and Chu smiled.

"This is easier than I expected. He said pride fully. So, this is an example of the best that Nightshade offers? Pathetic!"

He turned to his lieutenant and told him to wait outside with the drivers. After he left, Chu returned his focus to Graywolf. His body still lay on the floor in a puddle of water.

Chu raised his arms and began the power words to push the fire from his palms, but suddenly a grey mist appeared and swirled around him like a small tornado. A deep, sinister voice emerged from the surrounding mist. As fiery eyes peered through, Chu knew it was Asmodeus. I have returned on the day and the hour of the end of our bargain. Your allotted time is up and we come to collect.

Chu pleaded. "But I just need more time. Can we not renegotiate the deal?"

Asmodeus returned with an emphatic no! Then

the demon said with a final tone.

"Our bargain, now concluded, and so is our relationship."

In that moment, Graywolf opened his eyes long enough to see Chu come apart. Chu screamed as cracks appeared. A bright red fire emerged from all parts of his body until his body exploded into a thousand pieces, scattering across the room. Graywolf collapsed into unconsciousness again. The fire from Chu's demise spread throughout the warehouse until completely engulfed in flames.

The lieutenant got into one limo and spoke.

"We have to leave now!"

The driver responded.

"What about the master?"

The lieutenant answered back.

"I'm the master now!"

The two limos sped away as the lieutenant viewed the blaze through the rear window and smiled.

Epilogue

With Doctor Fu Wan Chu's sudden demise. There was a great relief that the horror of his reign was finally over. Though it was a mystery, such a powerful foe could crumble, seemingly with none of Nightshade's efforts or any plausible explanation.

The lieutenant stated simply in a meeting of the Shadow warriors.

"Fortunately, we can close the chapter of Chu's reign of terror and move on to stabilizing and reducing the possibility of anyone else rising to the occasion to lead the Triads. It is unfortunate that one of our brethren warriors lost his life in the battle with Doctor Chu. We miss Graywolf very much. He honored us all with his sacrifice. I believe we have witnessed the dawn of Hydra and its decline, thanks to Graywolf. Our continued efforts to fight crime whenever and wherever it arises will cause remnants of Hydra to fade into the sunset, never to rise again."

"So, perhaps providence has played a role here."

www.ingramcontent.com/pod-product-compliance
Lightning Source LLC
Chambersburg PA
CBHW070430120726
47910CB00003B/718